Charged with high █████████████████████████
London on suspicio████████████████████████
Plot, Philip Bloun████████████████████████
fiancée Honoria So████████████████████████
his release lies with Sir Gavin Hamilton, a handsome
Scottish courtier, the King's favourite. The ruthless Sir
Gavin, instantly attracted to Honoria, offers her Philip's
life for her honour. She rejects him only to be told that
he will move heaven and earth to bring about her
downfall.

To his surprise, he is unable to carry out these threats.
And why does the prospect of his marriage to the
influential Lady Philomena Sidney suddenly lose
enchantment? Can it be that he needs love more than all
the things he had fought for—power, wealth and the
King's favour?

By the same author in Masquerade

CAPTAIN BLACK
MAN WITH A FALCON

The King's Favourite
Caroline Martin

MILLS & BOON LIMITED
London · Sydney · Toronto

First published in Great Britain 1982
by Mills & Boon Limited, 15–16 Brook's Mews,
London W1A 1DR

© Caroline Martin 1982

Australian copyright 1982
Philippine copyright 1982

ISBN 0 263 73821 3

04/0482/

Set in 10 on 11 pt Times Roman

Photoset by Rowland Phototypesetting Ltd
Bury St Edmunds, Suffolk
Made and printed in Great Britain by
Cox & Wyman Ltd, Reading

CHAPTER
ONE

THE cold November rain turned the rutted road to mud beneath the hooves of a band of horsemen riding grimly east towards the scattered hamlet close to the Northamptonshire border.

But in the parlour of Lower Kilworth Manor the windows were curtained against the wet darkness and the three occupants had pulled their chairs close to the wide hearth. The firelight flickered kindly over the room, leaving in shadow the threadbare hangings, the much-mended chair covers, the well polished scratches on the worn furniture; lighting only, with the help of a single candle, the glowing auburn of Honoria's hair as she worked at her sewing, the shining fairness of her step-cousin Philip's bent head, and his long fingers turning the pages of a small leather-bound book, the closed eyes and open mouth of Aunt Anne as she slept unashamedly in her carved chair between the two of them.

It was a little haven of quiet against the roar of the wind and the battering of the rain upon the window, the only sounds the gentle splutter of logs on the fire and the rustle of the slowly turning pages: Aunt Anne was a peaceful sleeper.

After a time Honoria raised her head, and smiled across at Philip as his brown eyes met hers through the firelight. It was good to have him home again. Even though he had returned almost a month ago, she still felt a quiet glow of contentment from time to time, thinking of it. And in three weeks they would be married, as they had always known they would be one day, sooner or later. The secret ceremony in the tiny makeshift chapel under the eaves of the house would bring their life-long affection to its natural and inevitable conclusion.

'Will Robin Catesby be home in time to wish us well at our wedding?' Honoria asked. An old friend of theirs, Catesby's good looks and charm were an asset to any gathering.

She saw a small uncharacteristic frown gather between Philip's fair brows.

'I don't know,' he said slowly. 'I haven't seen him since he rode over just after I came home.'

And that was when, Honoria remembered suddenly, Philip had been troubled and abstracted for several days afterwards. What had the older man said to him, when they rode out together that day, which had left him so uneasy? Philip had told her it was nothing, and she had known better than to question him further, but it had worried her from time to time since then. Now she put the anxiety from her mind and said:

'Where is he, then?'

'In London, I heard. But I'm not sure.' He smiled, and all trace of the frown vanished. 'We shall be happy, whoever is there. We've learnt that from life at least, to expect nothing and to be grateful for what we have, however little.'

Which was true enough, Honoria thought. The struggle to survive had killed her father at last, as his estates dwindled steadily under the increasing burden of his fines. For herself and Philip it would be no easier, but they knew better perhaps what they must face. Though even for them there had been disappointment. Two years ago, when the Scottish King James had succeeded to the English throne, many people of their faith had hoped for greater toleration from the son of the Catholic Mary Queen of Scots. But they had soon learned their mistake. The penal laws remained in force: the restrictions on their movements, the fines for non-attendance at the parish church, the severer punishments for harbouring priests, even for converting others to the old faith. And it was said that the Parliament meeting this month in London would bring in still harsher laws against the Catholics.

'We must be patient,' Philip had said, many times. 'One day they will learn we mean no harm, that there is no danger to the kingdom in what we believe. Then things will get better.'

But it might be a long time yet, and whatever the future held for Philip and Honoria it was unlikely that material comfort would play much part in it.

Still, they had each other; and a roof over their heads—even if it was badly in need of repair, and a fire to sit beside, and the loving companionship of Philip's stepmother, Anne Blount, sister to Honoria's dead father, and three devoted servants who would stay with them even if there were no money left to pay their wages.

A log fell in a shower of sparks on to the hearth and Aunt Anne woke with a start, reaching for her spectacles and her sewing and trying to pretend she had never been asleep. Then, as Philip knelt to rearrange the fire they heard faintly, above the wind and the rain, the dull thunder of the approaching hooves. Along the road, turning into the Manor Lane, halting suddenly somewhere out there beyond the window.

Honoria looked up sharply.

'Horses? At this time of night?'

Philip's eyes met hers calmly, but his glance did nothing to quieten the anxious thudding of her heart. She went quickly to the window and pulled the curtain a little to one side.

She could see the horsemen easily enough, for they had lanterns, eerily illuminating the tired weather-beaten faces beneath the steel helmets. She could not see how many there were, for they stretched out of sight in both directions, taking up their positions, alert and watchful, as the hammering resounded on the door.

'Soldiers, Philip!' she whispered, white to the lips. 'A great company of them. What can it mean?'

Old Tom must have opened the door, for they heard voices now in the hall, courteous but firm in reply to Tom's mild protest.

'Stay here,' said Philip quietly. 'I'll go and see what they want.'

But Honoria followed him as he left the room, watching from the doorway as he crossed the hall to greet the man who stood there. She knew who it was at once: Sir Richard Verney, Sheriff of Warwickshire, a neighbouring landowner who had no love for Catholics. But he was a fair man, and they had never had reason to fear him, until now.

Her thoughts raced, tumbling over one another in panic. Why? Why this large armed force at their door, at this late hour? Unpaid fines would never merit that show of strength. There was no priest in the house, and had not been for months now . . .

'I must ask you to come with me, Master Blount,' Sir Richard was saying. 'There are certain questions—'

'Come with you?' broke in Honoria. 'But why? Philip has done nothing wrong!'

'Hush,' said Philip gently. 'Leave us, Honoria.'

But Sir Richard was already answering her question, his voice grimly incisive.

'Mistress Somervell, the state is in the gravest danger. It is a matter of high treason which brings me here.'

'Treason!' Instinctively, Honoria shrank back. She could see Philip's face, still and white: almost, she thought with a chill, as if he had half-expected the terrible word.

'Now,' went on the Sheriff briskly, 'my men must make a thorough search. You will wait together in there meanwhile: yourselves and the servants. There is no possibility of escape. We have the house surrounded.'

So they waited, gathered together in the parlour with a soldier on guard at the door, while the searchers tramped and thudded and banged overhead. Honoria stood in silence, with her hand in Philip's, and longed to question him, but she dared not, with hostile ears to overhear what she said. He seemed to be absorbed in some sober private thoughts of his own, remote from her. Aunt Anne had pulled out her rosary and was sliding the beads through her fingers, her eyes closed and a frown of concentration on her old face. That defiant act of faith would not help them in the eyes of the watchful guard, Honoria thought, but she could not intervene. Perhaps it would count for little either way, if already they thought Philip guilty of treason.

Treason! She shivered, and clasped his hand more firmly in hers. How could they think it of him, when he had lived quietly here all his life since his father died—all, that is, except those few months this year which he had spent in Flanders. Was that it, then? Did they suspect him of some intrigue while he had been away, taking the son of a widowed friend to school at the English Jesuit College at St Omers—that was against the law, of course, but it was not high treason. Was there indeed something which he had kept from her on his return, something which had brought Sir Richard to their door tonight?

His face told her nothing, even when at last he smiled at her, though she knew he was trying to bring her comfort.

'Do not be afraid, Honoria,' he said softly. 'All will be well, in the end.'

She longed to ask him how he could be sure, to ask if he knew why they suspected him. But she knew the guard had listened to every word which Philip had spoken. If only she could be sure that the answer to any question she asked would be so innocent that it would not matter who heard it.

'Look after mother,' he went on.

'You know I will, but surely you will be back very soon—tomorrow even—'

'If I am not, then. There is no way of telling. But you will be patient, I know.'

She wanted to cry out to him that she could not be patient, knowing nothing, understanding nothing, with that charge hanging over him. Then she thought: perhaps there is no question of implicating him in the affair, whatever it is; only that they think he can help them with their inquiries.

But before she could ask, in an undertone too low for the guard to hear clearly, the door was flung wide and two soldiers came to take him away, elbowing their way roughly into the room. She had time only to reach up swiftly for his brief final kiss before they marched him into the darkness beyond her sight. They took old Tom along, too, though she was not sure why. She ran after him, longing for some last word, some hope, some explanation. The front door swung closed in her face, orders were shouted beyond it, the soldiers clattered away into the night with their prisoners; and Honoria was left to turn and face her aunt in the silence which had so abruptly fallen.

They looked at each other without a word, numbed by the shock: there did not seem to be anything to say. It had all been so sudden, so entirely unexpected; and so appalling. Around them, wherever they looked, lay the utter disorder which the searchers had left: chairs and tables and stools overturned, broken, scattered, hangings torn from the walls, locked doors forced wide, pictures thrown to the floor, torn beyond repair, clothing pulled from the clothes presses and lying there in untidy heaps among books and candlesticks and utensils. They had left nothing, nothing at all, untouched.

'Well,' said Aunt Anne at last, without expression, beyond a note of overwhelming weariness. 'We've work to do, Honoria my dear.'

It was well into the night before some kind of order had been restored. Even then they knew that some things would never be the same again. In places the panelling itself had been dragged from the wall in the search for concealed rooms. Mercifully, the Manor's one priests' hole had been built by a master of his art, and they had not found it. It was not often used, but had twice saved precious lives.

When at last they could do no more, and the servants had gone to bed, Honoria said goodnight to her aunt and made her way slowly and wearily to her own room. It was cold and dark and cheerless—only sickness justified a fire anywhere but in parlour or kitchen—and she felt suddenly very alone.

If only they knew why all this had happened, had some idea what Philip was facing now! She knelt by the window and tried to pray, but felt herself grow only steadily colder and more weary. Yet when at last she went to bed she could not sleep, her thoughts tangled and disordered, leading nowhere but to increasing wakefulness.

Aunt Anne did not sleep much either; and the two women rose at last to a dark and cheerless morning and the knowledge that there must still be many hours of waiting before they could hope for any news. The wind and rain had subsided, giving way to a cold dripping mist which hung dismally around the house, shutting out daylight and cheerfulness with equal thoroughness. It was a relief when the evening came and they could light the candles and build up the fire in acknowledgement of the darkness.

And with the dark Tom came home, tired and stern faced.

They ran to meet him at the first sound of his horse on

the drive, and brought him in to the fireside and the welcome food and drink. Consideration kept them silent until he had taken his seat and eaten and drunk a little. And then at last they could contain themselves no longer.

'What's happened, Tom?' Honoria asked, with a gentle calmness of tone in which the tension she felt was scarcely audible. 'Why have you come back alone?'

'Because they let me come, Mistress Honoria,' said Tom. 'I couldn't tell them no more, so they'd no use left for me, I reckon.'

'What did they want you to tell them?' Aunt Anne asked sharply. 'What did they ask?'

'If I knew where Master Blount had been this summer, mistress. Which I didn't, as you know, and so I told them. I says I thought the Low Countries came into it somewhere, but that's all I could tell. Then—' he shifted uncomfortably in his chair—'then they asked about that time Master Catesby came over some weeks back—seems I'd been seen riding out with them that day—they said I must tell them what had passed between them. All I could say was that Master Blount had sent me on an errand to Mill Farm when we'd been a mile or two on our way, and I heard nowt I could think worth speaking of. Which is the truth, Mistress Blount—'

Honoria felt cold, though the fire blazed at her side.

'Tom, what has Master Catesby to do with it? Did they say?'

'Not they, but I learned soon enough when they let me go and I fell to talking to some I met on the way. Leastways, I know why they want to know about him. Though there's little enough they can do now, I suppose, seeing as he's dead.'

'Dead! Master Catesby is dead?'

'Aye,' Tom nodded. 'Shot, over Staffordshire way, where they ran him to ground with the others—'

'Others? What others?' Honoria's patience gave way at last. 'Tom, for the love of God, tell us what's happened! Where is Philip? What do they want with him?'

Tom gazed at her with pity.

'It's bad, mistress. They discovered a plot in London—last Tuesday, I think it was. It seems that Master Catesby was the leader—they planned to blow up the House of Lords, with the King and Queen, and the Prince of Wales as they met together for the opening of Parliament. They were found out just in the nick of time. So Master Catesby's dead, and some others that was with him, and the rest taken. But they know there was others that knew of it, or maybe played some part . . .' He paused, his eyes saying what he could not put into words.

'Philip—' whispered Honoria, with a shiver.

'Aye.' Tom's voice was as low as hers, hoarse with the horror of what he was saying. 'They sent me back, mistress, to tell you. He's taken to London, to the Tower.'

CHAPTER
TWO

IT was impossible to think of Philip taking any part at all in a plot to destroy so many innocent lives. Her gentle courteous Philip, who would not have spoken harshly even to his worst enemy, who thought no man or woman, whatever their religion, beneath his care and concern? No! Honoria rose to her feet, her eyes wide, shaking her head fiercely against the implication of what Tom had told them. She would not, could not believe that Philip had a hand in that terrible conspiracy.

Yet he was a Catholic—'an obstinate Papist' in the eyes of the law—and a friend of Robert Catesby, and they had talked together one day—might that not be enough to condemn him? Honoria shivered, and came to a sudden decision.

'I shall go to London,' she said firmly.

Anne Blount, struck dumb with horror at Tom's account, found her voice again.

'No, Honoria!' she said, reaching out to lay a hand on her niece's arm. 'No, my dear. That would only be to put yourself in danger. And what good would it do?'

'I don't know,' said Honoria, an obstinate line appearing about her mouth, 'but if nothing else perhaps I can see Philip and hear the truth from him. I do not believe he is guilty. And maybe I can do more than that. Uncle William Somervell may be able to advise me: he knows London well, and the ways of the world.'

'Too well,' said William Somervell's sister, disapprovingly. 'I can't think either that he'll be pleased to see one of his undesirable Catholic kin hammering at his door. Particularly if he fears it may reflect on his good

name to be connected with a man under suspicion, as
Philip is—'

'Philip's no blood relation,' said Honoria briskly.
'And if Uncle William fears dishonour then he may be
the more ready to help me prove his innocence.'

'And how can you hope to do that?' Anne asked
despairingly.

'I don't know' said Honoria, 'but if there is a way, I
shall find it.'

So the next day saw Tom on his travels again, in the
darkness before dawn, mounted on the old brown nag
with Honoria riding pillion behind him. They carried
with them only a little food, less money, and Honoria's
one good gown. They would halt once on the way, at the
cheapest inn they could find.

It was an exhausting journey, and more than once
Honoria had to repress an inclination to wonder what
madness had driven her to set out on so desperate a
venture. She began to think that Aunt Anne had been
right to suggest that there was nothing she could usefully
do. But she was on her way, and nothing now would
make her turn back.

It had already been dark for several hours when Tom
and Honoria rode next day through the narrow stinking
streets of London and halted in the chill fog before
William Somervell's prosperous town house. The
servant who admitted them with a great show of
reluctance was clearly deeply suspicious of them, in spite
of Honoria's forceful assertion that she was Master
Somervell's niece. It was not until they were standing in
the hall and her uncle had come down the stairs to meet
them, that the servant relaxed and left the mud-stained
and dishevelled travellers to the care of his master.

'Well, well, well!' said William Somervell, his plump
rosy face lit by a cheerful smile. 'Little Honoria, after all
this time!' He stood back a pace or two, to study her the
more carefully. 'Not so little, either: tall, like your

mother, I see. And quite as pretty, I'd say, under all that grime.' He reached out and took her cold hand in his, patting it affectionately. 'Now what brings you to my door in this bleak night, my girl?'

Honoria felt suddenly ridiculously close to tears. Perhaps it was the unexpected warmth of his welcome which had undermined her calmness, or her weariness after the long journey, or a delayed reaction to all that had happened during the last three days. Perhaps it was all three, or even the astonishing contrast of William Somervell's circumstances with her own.

She knew her uncle had turned his back as a young man on the inevitable hardships of the Catholic way of life chosen by the rest of his family. He had left home and settled in London, marrying a rich Protestant widow, who had since died, and attending the worship of the established church sufficiently often to keep in with the authorities. And he had done very well for himself as a consequence. Only once had he visited his brother at Kilworth, when Honoria was a small child, soon after Philip and his stepmother came to live with them. It had been a brief and painful experience. To the other Somervells, daily facing the consequences of their loyalty to their faith, William was a traitor. Yet now, looking round at the comforts of glowing fires and polished floors and comfortable furniture, and the innumerable little touches of luxury on every side, Honoria felt, just for a moment, that she could understand what had driven her uncle to it. She could understand; but she would not have chosen his way.

She swallowed her tears and said shakily:

'They have taken Philip to the Tower.'

At that all trace of humour left her uncle's face, and he became deeply serious.

'You'd better come in by the fire and tell me about it.'

Tom was sent to find food and rest in the kitchens, and William led Honoria into a snug parlour. The fire he spoke of was clearly the vast glowing hearth in here, not the equally welcoming one which had greeted them in the hall.

'Well,' he said at last, when she was seated in a comfortable chair with a glass of wine in her hand, and he had ordered food to be brought, 'tell me all about it.'

So she told him, grateful for his quiet but sympathetic attention to what she said; though she could see how much it shocked him. Clearly the news of the plot had already made a great impression on him, even before she arrived and revealed how closely it touched him.

When she had finished he gazed at her in silence for a moment or two, and then shook his head.

'That doesn't sound very good, Honoria. They would not have brought him all this way without good reason.'

'But he can't be guilty! It would be against all he believes—all he is.'

'May be. But it would be enough if he'd known of the existence of the plot and said nothing to the authorities. Is that possible, do you think?'

She remembered that ride with Robert Catesby, and his anxiety afterwards, and gazed miserably at her uncle.

'I don't know,' she whispered.

'Well, there's nothing we can do about it tonight. I'd be right in supposing you came to London to help young Philip? Is there any point in my asking if you had permission from the authorities to come?'

'No, I just came.'

He shook his head again.

'So I feared. Honoria, it's not wise at any time for known Catholics to go journeying far from home without leave, and at the moment—! Well, you can imagine how they'll be on the look out for any breach of the regulations. And if Philip's in the Tower, then you can be sure they'll have their eyes on you too, just in case. I imagine Lord Salisbury himself knows by now that you're sitting by my fire here.'

The Secretary of State, and most powerful man in the land: Honoria shivered.

'I'm sorry,' she said numbly. 'I hadn't thought.'

'It's you I was thinking of. However, that can't be helped, but now you're here, be guided by me—that's if you want my help?—though God knows what you think I can do.'

'I hoped you might have some advice for me. And I should like to see Philip, if I can.'

He nodded.

'I'll give some thought to it, and we'll talk again in the morning. Ah!' he looked round as a servant came in, 'here's your supper. Food and rest are what you need most.'

Later, when they were alone again and she had begun to eat, he said: 'You were to marry young Philip, weren't you? At least, your father had some such notion years ago.'

'Yes,' she said quietly. 'We were to be married at the end of this month.'

'Hmph,' was her uncle's only comment, before he changed the subject slightly. 'How's my sister Anne, then? She'll be taking this hard, I imagine. She always loved the lad as if she'd given birth to him herself—maybe the more because she had none of her own.'

'Yes, I think he means everything to her, and she's very dear to both of us. Oh, uncle, it has all happened so quickly and so suddenly and I don't know what to do!' And at that the long-suppressed tears rushed to her eyes and she bent her head on her hands, sobbing bitterly. William laid a gentle hand on her shoulder.

'There now, lass. We'll find a way out, never fear.' Which was a promise he was by no means sure he could keep, but was the only comfort he had to offer at the moment.

*   *   *

Honoria rose from her large and comfortable bed the next morning tired and troubled still, but a good deal calmer. She found over breakfast that her uncle had done more than sleep that night, for he had some suggestions to make.

'Now,' he said briskly, 'I'm not saying it'll get young Philip released, but it can't do you any harm to find yourself a friend at Court.'

Honoria's eyes widened.

'At Court? But how on earth can I do that?'

'Ah, there are ways, my dear. A word in the right place, a pretty face like yours raised in supplication—though by all accounts you're the wrong sex to move the King overmuch. And it wouldn't be easy for one of your religion to gain access to him just at present. Which means winning over one of those who have his ear. Money can help, but not, I think, in this case—besides, you've none, I imagine, and despite appearances I haven't much to spare. I'm comfortable, yes, but—' He caught her eye, and smiled. 'Back to the matter in hand: Salisbury's the most powerful man in the kingdom, without doubt—always excepting the King himself, and sometimes I wonder about that. But he'll be out to spread the net wider, not to let any suspect slip through his fingers. That's not to say he's incorruptible, but on this matter—well! No, on reflection, I think Sir Gavin Hamilton would be your best line of attack.' He smiled at her blank expression. 'The name means nothing to you? He wouldn't like that—one of the King's Scottish favourites. The fact that, like all the Scots, he's not much liked by the English at Court might make him more sympathetic to your case—*might*, but that's as much as I can say. It's worth a try. Certainly, he has the King's favour, and wealth and honours enough to prove it. They say, too, that whatever qualities the King admires in him, he has an eye for a pretty woman.' He looked her up and down. 'Have you a decent gown with you? Good. Jane Porter, my housekeeper—' Honoria was shocked to see him wink broadly, implying that the relationship was closer than the word suggested '—can go with you. A sensible woman. Now go and beautify yourself, and I'll have the coach brought to the door. No sense in wasting time.'

CHAPTER
THREE

Sɪʀ Gavin Hamilton was bored.

Around him in his splendid house in the Strand were ranged all the trappings of luxury: the finest furniture, exquisite pictures and hangings and ornaments—things which in his impoverished boyhood he would never have dreamed of possessing. In an adjoining room a dinner large and sumptuous enough for ten would soon be laid ready for his sole enjoyment. In one part of the city or another, not far away, lived at least four beautiful women who would, he knew, come running at his slightest bidding. He had the favour of the King, and all the benefits of power and wealth which that bestowed. He had a vast household of servants, for whom he could scarcely find occupation enough. He had a substantial band of liveried and well-armed retainers, convenient both for his protection in the violent streets of London and to wreak whatever vengeance he required on his enemies. And he had freedom, as a bachelor without responsibilities to any but himself.

And for most inhabitants of London just now life had become perhaps a little too exciting. Even Sir Gavin had to admit that had his King been blown to whatever afterlife awaited him on that bleak November day last week, he might have found himself facing a very different future. The Scots who had followed their King to England on his accession were little liked, and with James dead they would be at the mercy of their enemies. All this magnificence, which at the moment bored him so intensely, would have vanished overnight.

But the plot had failed, and Gavin was not remotely

interested in the rounding up of the conspirators. The political and religious problems of England wearied him, except in so far as he could make use of them for his own ends.

So today he was bored. He ran his fingers over the shining keys of the beautifully-inlaid virginals; strummed idly on his lute, turned the pages of a couple of books before flinging them aside—he had acquired them for the splendour of their bindings rather than for their contents; changed his clothes three times, discarding one dazzling ensemble for another and then another, rode one of his magnificent horses for a while about the streets, with an entourage of retainers to proclaim his strength to the passers by, had his hair trimmed —unnecessarily—by his barber, and sent a man to bring a selection of rings in from the goldsmith, so that he might choose one which took his fancy. He was standing at the window of his vast banqueting hall, staring moodily out at the beautiful rain-washed garden which sloped away towards the river, when a servant brought word that Mistress Honoria Somervell and her woman begged an interview with him.

The name meant nothing to him, which suggested either that they had never met, or that she was supremely unmemorable. Probably the latter, he thought gloomily. But he welcomed any diversion, and ordered the man to show her in. Women who called to see him fell into two categories, he had found, whatever their ostensible reason for being there. Either they sought his influence on behalf of some private wrong, or they hoped to end the day in his bed—which they rarely did, since he preferred to make his own choices in that delicate matter. But if this Mistress Somervell had brought her woman along for company, then most likely she had no designs of that kind.

And then she was there, facing him across the smooth shining boards of the floor, and all speculation was driven from his head by the startling unexpectedness of her appearance.

She was about twenty perhaps, tall and slender, dressed in a sombre gown of black velvet relieved only by the stark whiteness of the neat ruff at her throat and the delicate silver crucifix which unwisely proclaimed her faith to the world. The dark richness of the gown set off to perfection the creamy oval of a lovely face, framed in a shining mass of auburn hair, glowing like fire beneath the diaphanous lawn of the hood which adorned it. A small rosy mouth, firm but perfect in shape, a straight nose, delicate dark brows arched above clear eyes, wide and long-lashed. No, he had not met Honoria Somervell before. If he had he would not have forgotten her in a million years. And if it lay in his power he would make sure that she had reason to remember this meeting.

He took a deep breath, to dispel the strange dizziness which seemed to have assailed him; curved his fine mouth into the smile of dazzling charm which never failed to overcome the most resistant of ladies—or win whatever favour he chose from the susceptible King—and advanced towards her, hand outstretched in welcome.

'Mistress Somervell, I should be honoured to learn how I may be of service to you.'

He found himself gazing into those incredible eyes, and for a few seconds his self-possession abandoned him again. Grey-green, within the smoky fringe of dark lashes, flecked intriguingly with gold and blue and brown, eyes which offered so many possibilities, so many moods, so many delights—and which now were full only of a daunting directness, cool and purposeful, as if she were wholly unaware of anything but her reason for being here. As yet, it seemed, the infallible charm had not worked.

But he had been too disturbed himself at his first sight

of her to notice that she had not after all been entirely unaware of his splendour. As he had gazed at her in a kind of awe, Honoria for her part had forgotten completely for a moment why she was here. She did not know what kind of man she had expected to meet; but she had been entirely unprepared for the astonishing magnificence of his appearance. Tall, powerfully made but lean, his hair curling crisply golden brown over his arrogant head, his eyes vividly blue, dressed in doublet and hose of dazzling tawny velvet, embroidered with gold and silver thread, he was like no other man she had ever met. She had felt an odd sensation in the pit of her stomach and had only just managed to recollect herself and retrieve her wandering concentration when he came towards her, speaking in a voice as richly masculine as his appearance.

But by now she had remembered Philip, and his plight, and this man she faced was simply someone who might help them both.

'Sir,' she said, in the deep and melodious voice which had gone largely unappreciated by those around her, who had heard it almost every day of their lives. 'Sir, I come to beg your help and support on behalf of my most dear cousin, Master Philip Blount.'

'My most dear cousin'—he didn't like that; but the charming untroubled smile remained, and he asked, the words attractively accented:

'And in what way do you suppose I may assist your cousin?'

'He . . . he is in the Tower, sir.' He could see those lovely eyes brimming with tears, all for another man. Bravely, she swallowed and went on: 'We were to have been married this month.'

Then she was single! His heart gave a small leap of satisfaction—and anticipation. Unwed, and presumably a virgin. No one, as yet, had been afforded the exquisite privilege of carrying her to bed, unloosing the laces of that severely seductive gown, touching the white smooth flesh beneath, seeing those sweet lips part in expectant passion. . . His eyes travelled over her, feeding his excited imagination, and then reached her face again, and those coolly disapproving eyes. It was almost as if she read his thoughts, and for the first time in years he blushed. It was a moment or two before he was again the smooth courtier, urbanely giving audience to a humble supplicant.

He led her to a brocaded chair beside one of the long windows and encouraged her to talk, gravely attentive, though his thoughts were absorbed less by her tale than by the rise and fall of her musical voice, the changing emotions of her expressive eyes. Even so he missed nothing in her account of Philip's misfortune which might be useful to him, later, when he had allowed himself time for reflection.

When she had finished he stood gazing down at her, his face thoughtful.

'I think, Mistress Somervell,' he said carefully, 'that I may be able to assist you. But I must give the matter some thought, and perhaps question you further. Will you do me the honour of dining with me, so that we may talk while we eat?'

Honoria was struck only by the warm sympathy of his tone, the appearance of deep concern for her trouble. She accepted his offer, waited while Jane Porter was courteously despatched to seek refreshment in the servants' quarters, and allowed him to lead her into an adjoining room, where a long table stood laden with food, and liveried servants hovered to wait on them.

The meal which followed opened up a new world to Honoria, facing her host across that lavish table. They ate and drank from gold and silver and crystal, dishes and goblets which must alone have cost more than all she possessed in the world. And on these exquisite utensils was laid an astonishing range of culinary delights, from the simplest but exquisitely delicate of venison pasties to fruits and meats she had never seen before, and whose delicious sweetness was beyond her wildest imaginings. Thinking of Philip's hardships she could never have appreciated what Sir Gavin placed before her, but, somehow, very soon, she ceased to think of Philip at all.

For the most astonishingly delightful aspect of that meal was her companion. She had never heard talk like that before, so alive, so worldly and yet considerate of her country standards, so full of wit and humour and brilliance, that she found herself laughing and chattering like a child, talking of herself and her home, carried out of herself by sheer enjoyment. At home the talk was always grave, serious, often scholarly, but their circumstances were such that light-heartedness, except of the simplest kind, was a rarity. For the first time in her life she gave herself up to enchanting frivolity, and was intoxicated. She quite forgot that he had asked her to dine so that they might talk of Philip.

She realised at last that they had come to the end. Not that the food was finished, or the wine: there was enough still to feed a poor man's household for a week. But she could eat no more, and Sir Gavin was leaning at ease in his chair, his fingers curled loosely about the stem of his glass, and they had fallen silent. He was smiling slightly as he watched her, a man at peace with the world.

'Now, Mistress Somervell,' he said at last, his tone full of languid contentment, 'I suggest we adjourn to the library and turn our minds to more serious matters.' His whole manner was so lacking in any suggestion of serious thought that it was a moment or two before Honoria realised what he meant, with a pang of conscience that she could have been so given up to light-hearted enjoyment while Philip languished in the Tower.

More sober now, she went with him across the banqueting hall where they had first met, onto the spacious gallery where a wide flight of stairs led down to the entrance hall, and—once he had brushed aside the man who waited with a gleaming tray of rings held out for his attention—into a room which led off it. The library was a charming room, on the first floor, with a view of trees and grass and the river with its passing traffic. Its walls were lined with lavishly bound volumes, and hung in the intervening spaces with fine pictures, its ceiling was of beautifully moulded plaster, and at intervals stood marble busts and statuettes, and a number of musical instruments—virginals, a lute on a fringed stool, a set of recorders in their satin-lined cases.

Sir Gavin crossed to the virginals and ran his fingers lightly over the ivory keys; and then turned to smile at Honoria.

'Are you fond of music, Mistress Somervell?'

'I know very little about it, sir,' she said quietly.

'Then I shall initiate you into its mysteries,' he said, and took his seat before the keyboard.

He did not play with any exceptional skill but with a vigour and enthusiasm which was like his conversation, so dazzling that one did not observe its imperfections. To Honoria, who had indeed no knowledge of music at all, it was entrancing. She moved to stand beside the instrument, watching the swiftly moving fingers, absorbed in the tinkling sweetness of the music.

After a time he moved on to a tripping, teasing tune, raised his blue eyes, full of gentle laughter, to her face, and began to sing.

'Shall I come, sweet love, to thee
When the evening gleams are set,
Shall I not excluded be—?'

Slowly, as he sang, the amusement faded from his eyes, and an intense gravity filled them, an intensity which held her gaze, so that she could not look away, so that she no longer thought even of the music, but only of him. She had never felt so strange before, breathless, oblivious to anything around her. It was as if she were suspended outside time and space, alone with him, drowning sweetly, painfully, in those blue eyes. The song dwindled to silence, his hands lay still on the keys. Slowly, almost imperceptibly, he rose to his feet and came to her side.

He was so close now . . . Honoria held her breath, her eyes never leaving his. A hand touched her arm, and with a slow, firm, inevitable movement slid to her waist, drawing her near, so that she felt his closeness, the hard strength of his body, the quickness of his breathing. Then the other hand raised her face to his and slid into the thickness of her hair. As if something within her drew her on she brought her mouth up to meet his. It was not a kiss, but a fierce meeting of their whole bodies. She felt it quiver through her, bringing her fiercely alive, to reach up and clasp him to her, crying out in silent longing for him to hold her and caress her and satisfy the desire which lit her so intensely. Her lips parted beneath his, she felt his hands move caressingly along the curve of her back, felt the sweet closeness of his strong body against hers.

And then, slowly, firmly, he drew back, his hands gently at her elbows. He was breathing fast still, his eyes darkened, watching her. Honoria reached blindly for a stool and sat down heavily before her trembling limbs should give way. What had happened to her just now? That sudden fierce flame of passion—her longing response to his glance and his touch—the desire within her still which set her heart beating so fast and almost drove her to reach out to him again. She had never felt like this before in all her life, not for one fleeting moment. She had not known she *could* feel like this, and the very power of her emotions disturbed and astonished her.

Slowly she linked her quivering hands together in her

lap, and tried to draw a deep breath. She raised her eyes
to the face of this man who had today opened so many
doors to her. She was not sure that she wished to move
into this unfamiliar world to which he seemed to be
calling her. She thought, longingly—and guiltily too—of
Philip: his gentleness, his calmness and dignity and
uncompromising principles. The colour flooded her face
as she imagined what he would think of her behaviour
today.

Yet this man had been kind: he had heard her with
sympathy, entertained her royally. Just now, perhaps,
he had been as helpless as she against the force of that
unexpected passion. She could not read his expression as
he stood there: it was grave and withdrawn, with the
traces still, as hers must have, of that moment of
indiscretion. He said nothing for a while, and when he
spoke his tone was harsh, abrupt, severe even. But his
actual words were entirely unexpected.

'I will do what I can for Master Blount.'

She gave a quick sharp intake of breath, her eyes
wide.

'On one condition,' he went on, and continued to gaze
at her.

She was so astonished at his sudden return to the
matter which had brought her here that for a moment or
two she could not find her voice.

'Thank you,' she stammered at last. 'I will do
anything—'

He gave an odd half-smile.

'So I hoped,' he said lightly, and came to her side. He
reached down and touched her cheek, a light caress
which sent a shiver of excitement leaping through her. 'It
is simple enough. All I require to ensure the release of
your betrothed is that you give me—' he touched her
again, and his voice fell to a whisper '—what I ask . . .'

What was in his eyes now brought the colour to her
cheeks and robbed her of all power of speech. She bent

her head, and felt his hand move entrancingly to the nape of her neck, slide under the edge of her ruff. She scarcely heard his next words, so softly were they spoken.

'You will come to my bed, tonight and every night, for as long as I require—until Master Blount is free—'

The spell was broken. In one swift movement of fierce indignation she rose to her feet, sending the stool clattering away from her, her lovely eyes sparkling with scornful anger.

'How dare you! How dare you even suggest so vile a thing! I see it all now—I thought you kind, generous, ready to help, but, thank God, my eyes are opened in time! I only wish I had been wise enough to see it at once, before I took my first step across your threshold. Send for my woman: I am going home!'

He was laughing now, actually laughing, though he became grave again as she finished speaking and moved to the door.

'Well done, sweeting! That was magnificent! Anger sets off your beauty to its greatest advantage—you should cultivate it! And by all means go home: I would not be the one to prevent you. But I shall be happy to do what I can to assure you of a good view for Master Blount's execution.'

She gasped at that, and stood quite still, ashen-faced.

'How can you!' she choked, her hands raised pathetically for a moment in an imploring gesture, and then falling again.

'Very easily,' he said. 'After all, you have not given serious thought to my proposition. It merits that at least, I feel.'

'Philip is innocent,' she said. 'They cannot condemn him.'

'He would not be the first innocent man to be hanged, drawn and quartered,' said Sir Gavin sharply. She shuddered, and closed her eyes for a moment as if to shut out the unbearable vision. And then opened them again as she heard his approaching steps. 'Come and sit down,' he said, laying a hand on her arm, 'and talk about this rationally.'

'Rationally!' she exclaimed, halfway between laughter and tears: though she went with him part of the way, adding: 'I shall not sit down again in your house.'

He gave a mocking half bow.

'As you please, mistress.' He himself resumed his seat on the stool beside the virginals, and touched a key or two reflectively. 'Let us see how we stand, then. Your Master Blount is in the Tower, it is possible he knew of the plot beforehand, it is also likely that there is no shred of evidence as to whether he did or not, beyond his word on it. And even that you have not had. If he knew of the plot and yet kept silent then he is as guilty as the others, and he will die. Even if he did not know, he will die, I imagine. Salisbury is not in a forgiving mood. Unless —unless, Mistress Somervell, I can put in a word on his behalf where it will do most good—and that I can do, if I choose. I would perjure myself if it suited me, you know.'

'I can believe it!' she said bitterly. He smiled with bland assurance, and went on:

'And I, Mistress Somervell, will be only too happy to speak that word, if you give me what I ask. What could be simpler?'

'You ask for my honour, and call it "simple"?'

'Your honour for his life, mistress. Which do you value most highly?'

'I . . . I think I know which Philip would hold more dear—'

'But it is not Philip who makes the choice, sweeting, is it? Besides, what am I asking of you after all? A night or so in my company, in my bed, in my arms—and I swear to you, mistress, you would delight in every long sweet moment of it—and afterwards, well, you marry your Philip and settle down to a life of virtuous matronliness as if nothing had happened. He need never know—I can be discretion itself, if I choose—'

'I have never had any secrets from Philip!'

He laughed.

'Then it's high time you began, sweeting. You'll have a tedious life, else—' He caught the sharp disapproval in her eyes, and his tone altered to a low caressing note: 'Come now, my dear—it is what you want, you know that. Just now, when I held you, and kissed you—you did not hold back then. I could have had what I wanted, and more—'

She blushed furiously.

'You have no right to argue from my moment of weakness. I hope I have moral sense enough to know the difference between lust and lawful passion. And if that's what you think, why didn't you take what you wanted then?'

'Because I don't want it that way, sweeting. And I don't want you once only. I want you as my mistress until you go home for your marriage—and I want you to come of your own free will.'

'Free! When you bargain for Philip's life?'

'Relatively free,' he corrected. He smiled. 'I think I offer an irresistible bargain.'

'Then God have mercy on your vile soul!' she exclaimed. 'And on me,' she added, 'for I'm punished enough for that weakness of mine just now—' She turned to him: 'I am going home.'

His eyes flashed suddenly with anger.

'You Catholic women are all the same—cold as nuns at heart!' he said unpleasantly.

'What are your Protestant women, then? Whores?'

He laughed at that, with rueful delight.

'Oh, my dear, I must have you, if it's the last thing I do—'

'Never!' she said, and walked grim faced from the room.

As he watched her go the reluctant admiration in his eyes gave way to anger, and resolution. He was not used to being thwarted. And he had never, he thought, wanted anything as much as he wanted her. Somehow, if he had to move heaven and earth to do it, he would have her, on his own terms.

He turned to the window and gazed out at the distant view of the swiftly flowing river, frowning, and deep in thought.

CHAPTER
FOUR

ONE look at his niece's white face as she returned to the house that day told William Somervell that all had not gone well with her visit to Sir Gavin Hamilton. Her beautiful eyes glowed dark in the surrounding pallor, burning with anger and misery, their colours submerged by her conflicting emotions. With an instinctive gesture of sympathy he took her hand in his and held it, gazing at her inquiringly.

'No good then, my girl?'

She shook her head, and tiny sparkling points of light seemed to dart briefly in the depths of her eyes.

'He is an evil man, uncle, hateful and evil. No good can ever come of anything he does.'

Her uncle sighed.

'Still, I had hoped—sometimes evil tools can be used for good ends, and no one can deny his power—but there, never mind now. At least we tried. Come in and dry yourself, and we'll think what's to be done.'

But she did not want to sit at the fireside endlessly discussing ways and means, or suffering her uncle's soothing platitudes. She wanted desperately to be alone. As soon as she could she excused herself and went up to the spacious guest bedroom, to stand at the window gazing out at the rain. Very much, did she but know it, as Sir Gavin was doing at this moment in another part of London.

Not that in any sense her thoughts bore any resemblance to his in their grim single-mindedness. In fact they were not clear at all, for the stern dignity which had graced her exit from his house had masked a tumultuous confusion of emotions. Now, alone in her room, they overwhelmed her. Fury was uppermost, for how dared he? How dared he make so vile a suggestion to her, how dared he play with her deepest feelings of love and loyalty for his own ends, using her, manipulating her?

And then in the next moment she grew hot with shame, for she knew that if she had not allowed him to lead her so far he would not have found her so ready a tool, not perhaps have made that humiliating offer. Her anger was not all directed towards him. Some of it was turned on herself, on that weak, wayward woman lurking somewhere within the depths of her being, whom he had sought out and played upon as skilfully, as effortlessly as his fingers had brought music from the creamy keys of the virginals.

'God forgive me . . .' she whispered, head bent in shuddering humiliation. And even as she spoke her capricious thoughts conjured up again the touch of his hand on her neck, the force of his mouth on hers . . .

She threw up her head sharply, eyes closed, and remembered Philip. Dear Philip, who loved her so well, and understood her, and cared for her—and she for him. After all that had happened he was no nearer to safety, no nearer to returning to his home, to his stepmother, to her, and their long-awaited marriage.

'He wouldn't be the first innocent man to be hanged drawn and quartered.' Softly she cried out now, remembering those words. Then inexorably Sir Gavin's voice seemed to say again: 'Your honour for his life—which do you value most highly?' His life, said her heart at once, for what is honour if he is dead? Dead at my hands, as surely as if I had tied the noose, because I could have saved him.

But the price of his life was to yield to that hateful man, allow him to use her as he would. Not just the hand at her neck, the lips on hers, but more, far more, other things which she could not imagine. She could only guess—and she knew that the thudding beat of her heart was not caused by fear, or anxiety for Philip, or even by shame . . .

She fell to her knees and drew the rosary from the concealed place in her sleeve and began feverishly to pray.

'Give me strength, please give me strength!'

But strength for what? She did not know. It was not that she doubted what Philip's choice would be: she had known that at once, without hesitation. He would not want her to make that sacrifice. But perhaps he was wrong: her honour was such a little thing set against the dreadful death which threatened him. Surely it could not be right to be so coldly virtuous that she should choose to destroy him rather than yield? If it had been her own life the choice would have been easy, for all her instruction from her earliest years had taught her that chastity was the highest of virtues.

By supper time she was no nearer finding an answer to the questions which haunted her. She ate little, scarcely heard what was said to her, and went to bed to lie awake through the long hours of the night, gazing at the delicate plasterwork of the ceiling, seeing nothing. Tomorrow she must decide. Tomorrow she must try one of her uncle's suggestions, without real hope of success, or go home, back to safety, leaving Philip to his fate, or she must go in secret to that splendid house and tell Sir Gavin that she would do all he asked, if only he would have Philip set free.

It would all be so very much easier, she knew, if some part of her did not thrill with hopeful, forbidden excitement at the thought of what he might do to her.

When morning came at last her thoughts were as confused as ever. She ate little breakfast, and afterwards paced the house in nervous uncertainty, her eyes heavy with sleeplessness, her limbs weary but unable to find rest. In the end she knew she must have air: outside in the cold grey morning she might be able to think more rationally. Jane Porter was setting out for market, and Honoria pulled a heavy cloak over her worn country gown, and joined her.

Outside she did not find that her problems miraculously solved themselves, but at least there were distractions from her anxieties. The street in front of her uncle's house was already thronged with people and traffic, so that the passing carts and wagons and coaches could scarcely move for the crowds. The noise, to one accustomed to country quietness, was deafening. The stench, of unwashed bodies jostling one another, of rubbish tipped from adjoining houses to lie underfoot, of the thick clogging smoke from a thousand household coal fires, was almost unbearable even on this cold day—what it must be like in summer Honoria shuddered to think. Most of all, the things she saw about her set her glancing this way and that in innocent wonder. Yesterday in the pouring rain there had been few people about, and she and Jane had kept heads bent against the weather for the short distance from coach to door. Today the townsfolk were out in force: men, women and children of all kinds, rich and poor, diseased and healthy, ugly and beautiful alike.

Across the street, facing her uncle's house, a man caught her eye: short but broad-shouldered, his pink pock-marked face contrasting strangely with the bleached lightness of hair and eyes. She shivered, and looked away to find some more acceptable sight. Her eyes fell instead on a woman, hair dyed and curled, face painted, gown cut so scandalously low that her breasts showed, firm and pink-nippled above the satin bodice. Honoria blushed uncomfortably and turned to watch a small boy skilfully bowling his hoop through the jostling crowds. Then Jane tugged at her arm to hurry her along, and they plunged into the mêlée, pushing and shoving,

dragged and pulled this way and that by passers by, until
Honoria realised with sudden panic that Jane had
disappeared from sight.

She stood still, glancing agitatedly around, searching
the passing faces, ahead and behind, from side to side.
Some way back she caught sight of the pock-marked
man, coming slowly her way. He paused as her gaze
reached him, and then was lost to sight. There were
other women like the one she had seen, their bodies
brazenly displayed. With a sense of shock it dawned on
her that they could not all be the prostitutes she had
taken them for, since some were richly dressed,
respectfully accompanied by servants and parents. It
was a relief to see a severely-dressed Puritan housewife
in grey homespun and unstarched ruff, modestly on her
way to market, or the respectable city matron in the
fashions of twenty years ago taking the air with an
elderly maid for company. But there was no sign of Jane:
all those faces, and none of them was familiar!

She had almost decided to give up and go home when
her arm was grasped from behind and she saw with relief
that Jane had returned in search of her. After that, she
clasped the housekeeper's arm firmly with one hand and
clung on despite the pressing throng.

When they reached the market things were a little
easier. The crowds moved more slowly, the traffic
passed to one side of the stalls. But the noise, with every
stall-holder shouting his wares, was more deafening than
ever. She followed Jane as she went from stall to stall,
buying here, rejecting there, selecting the best in fruit
and vegetables: although, Jane explained, they should
have been up before dawn to be sure of the highest
quality. Only the second rate was left now.

While Jane bargained with this stall-holder and that,
Honoria paused and looked about her, marvelling at the
unheard-of range and variety of goods displayed,
amused by the shouts of the sellers, the fierce arguments

over apples or eggs, shocked again and again by the squalor and degradation of so much she saw about her.

Then she saw the pock-marked man again, standing in an ale-house doorway across the street. She was sure that his eyes had moved away from her as she saw him, that he had been watching her. She felt a little inexplicable quiver of fear. But how foolish, she thought. He has as much right as I to come to market and watch the crowds. She was glad all the same when Jane moved on to another stall and they could no longer see him.

As they walked home again, the shopping completed, she felt more than once that watchful eyes were on her from somewhere in the crowded streets. Several times she turned: twice she saw him again, some distance behind, not looking her way.

'Jane,' she said at last, nervously, 'I think that man is following us.'

She turned to point him out to her companion, but he was nowhere to be seen. Jane laughed.

'Then he'll lose us soon enough, I'll be bound. But it'll be chance that brings him this way, you can be sure of that. He'd not get far trying to follow anyone in this crowd.'

Even so, Honoria was relieved when they reached her uncle's house at last and the front door closed behind her, shutting out the exhausting clamour of the streets. She would not be anxious to take the air again until she was safely back in the tranquility of the country-side.

Then she saw her uncle coming towards her, bright-eyed with excitement, an official-looking paper in his out-stretched hand.

'See here, Honoria, perhaps Sir Gavin Hamilton is not so bad after all. One of his men brought this round for you half an hour ago.'

She felt her colour rise at the name, and stood still where she was, half way across the hall.

'I want nothing he can offer,' she said, tight-lipped.

'Ah, but you'll want this. Come, see what it is.'

She came, reluctantly, and took it from him. But sleeplessness and anxiety and the experiences of the morning had bewildered her. She stood gazing at the paper, making no sense of the even, black official writing, the sprawled signature.

'What is it. . . ?' she asked at last. Her uncle snatched it back in exasperation.

'Can't you read, girl? It's a pass—a pass signed by the Lieutenant of the Tower. You can go and see young Philip. Now. Today.'

A bitter wind was blowing off the river as Honoria and her uncle came within sight of the Tower. But it was not that which caused the icy chill at her heart as she raised her eyes to the great flint-grey fortress which confronted them.

The Tower had for many generations been a place of horror, a dreadful symbol to many of her faith. Built as a residence for Kings, in the days when strong walls counted for more than wide airy rooms and cushioned comfort, it had for a long time now come to be a place of imprisonment, and torture, and death for the King's enemies. Honoria had expected to see a vast and impregnable stronghold, but she had not known it would cast over her so powerful an impression of evil. She seemed to see those grey stones drenched in blood, echoing to the cries of the innocent and the doomed, rising relentlessly before her against a sky as cold and impenetrable. And somewhere, deep within one of those towers, behind those brooding walls, Philip lay: never perhaps to emerge until the scaffold was built, the hangman ready—

Instinctively, she crossed herself, and reached to clasp her uncle's arm. He patted her hand reassuringly, disturbed by her pallor, and the wide eyes gazing in horror at the Tower. He hoped she would not find it all too much for her.

He led her gently to where the guard waited to examine her pass. After that, he knew, she must go on without him, leaving him fidgeting with anxiety while she followed softly at the heels of the guard.

It was a long way, deep into the Tower, along dark passages, up winding stairs, on and on. She could never have found her way alone. She had a nightmare fear, quickly suppressed, that she might be abandoned here, lost for ever in this twisting maze of corridors, that there was no way out . . .

But at last the guard halted at a heavy door, and called to another man, who came jangling his keys to glance at the pass and then to unlock the door.

'Half an hour, then,' said the first man. 'I'll come for you when it's time.'

And he pushed open the door.

She went in, her heart quickening with apprehension. What would she find? What might they have done to Philip through the past long days? She heard the door slam closed behind her, the key turn.

And then he had her hands in his, and was bending to kiss her gently on the forehead, and she was looking up into his quietly welcoming face. Through rising tears of relief and distress she saw that he was pale and tired, but calm, smiling that dear familiar smile in his gladness at seeing her.

'Honoria, dear Honoria, I had not expected . . .' he began, his voice a little unsteady with emotion.

She looked from him to the room: large enough, but dark, one high tiny window giving the only light. And damp—the stink of damp walls and damp rushes on the stone floor reached her nostrils, she could see the moisture glisten green on the stonework. A low hard bed and a stool, and an empty plate and cup were all the furniture the room contained. Rich men—even those charged with treason—could buy light, and a fire, and good food and comfort. But Philip was not a rich man.

Honoria swallowed hard, and gazed again into his beloved face.

'How have they used you, Philip?' she whispered. 'What . . . what have they done?'

He put a gently comforting arm about her and led her to the stool, to sit there looking up at him.

'I have not suffered torture, Honoria, if that's what you mean,' he answered quietly. 'I am, I think, more fortunate than others in this. No, I have nothing to complain of.'

Nothing to complain of! She glanced round her again, shuddering. Day after day, night after long night in this place—or did they take him somewhere else for questioning? And what ghastly sights and sounds haunted him when he was alone, to tell him that others suffered worse than this?

'What is happening? What will they do?'

He sat on the end of the bed nearest to her, and shook his head.

'I don't know. It's not in my hands. Don't look like that, Honoria. It is not like you to lose your courage. You must be brave, my dear.'

She bent her head to hide the unshed tears.

'I think I could be braver if I were here, in your place,' she said. And her heart added: 'I would do anything to free you—anything!' But she could not say it.

He laid a hand over hers.

'Now that's nonsense! You are much better able to care for the house, and Mother. How is she, Honoria? And how did you come to leave her?'

She felt that his question implied disapproval that she was not still at home with Aunt Anne, and she coloured slightly.

'She's well enough, Philip. But you know what you mean to her—'

'So you came to try and work a miracle and bring me home. Is that it?'

She looked up sharply.

'Would it take a miracle, Philip? Is it as bad as that? Philip, I wish I knew—'

He smiled wryly.

'So do I, Honoria. As it is I can offer you little comfort.'

'But what do they say?' she demanded. 'What do they charge you with? Have they questioned you?'

'Yes,' he replied. 'They asked about my trip to Flanders—and about Robin Catesby.'

'And what did you tell them?'

'The truth,' he answered steadily.

'But what is the truth?' she cried in anguish. Oh, if only she knew that there was nothing to fear, that he imagined his danger!

He took hold of her hands, looking gravely into her eyes.

'Honoria,' he said with an undercurrent of reproach in his voice, 'don't you trust me? Do *you* think I had a part in this terrible conspiracy?'

'I . . . I only know that you are here. But, Philip,' she went on more firmly, 'I could never believe that you would wish harm to any living soul, not even your greatest enemy. No, I don't believe you had a part in it. Only, if you knew of it—if Robin Catesby spoke of it that day . . .' She remembered his troubled face, the long silences which shut her out.

'I know,' he said. 'In that case I am equally as guilty, in the eyes of the law, as if I had been found standing at the side of poor Guy Fawkes in the vault beneath Parliament House. No, Honoria, I did not know. Robin told me no details of the plot—' He raised his hand to silence her as she was about to cry out with relief. 'But he did ask me what I would think if a group of bold men of our faith were to stake everything on a difficult and dangerous blow against the state. He gave no details, mentioned no names. He was sounding me out, I think, trying to gauge whether I might join them. When I made my feelings clear he said no more. That is all. But it is enough, I think, for their purposes.'

Honoria said nothing: she could think of nothing to say. Despair overwhelmed her. There was no hope, then. The King and his council would take their revenge as thoroughly, as implacably as lay in their power. Philip would die the horrible, agonising, lingering death of a traitor before the gloating eyes of Protestant London.

Unless . . . With a sudden movement, she rose to her feet and walked restlessly to stand beneath the tiny window, her back to Philip. Head bent over clasped hands, she thought: 'I must do it—I must . . . !' and did not know she had spoken aloud.

Philip came and placed his hands on her shoulders.

'Honoria . . . Honoria, what is it?'

'Nothing,' she said slowly, 'only . . . only there is someone who might help, if . . .' She broke off, and he turned her gently to face him, though she would not look up.

'Who is it?' he asked. She hesitated, and then said with rising colour:

'Sir Gavin Hamilton.'

He nodded thoughtfully.

'The King's current favourite—yes, he has great power, they say. But there are other things, too, I've heard about him. What makes you think he'd care what becomes of us? We have no great influence, you and I, Honoria.' He looked faintly amused at the very thought.

'I . . . I went to see him,' Honoria explained. 'It was he who sent me the pass to come here. I think—I know—he would help.'

For a moment or two he was silent, gazing down on her bent head. Then he placed a hand beneath her chin and raised it, so that she looked into his eyes.

'On what terms, Honoria?'

She blushed furiously.

'I said nothing about terms,' she objected.

'No, but I know you, my dear. And I know a little of the world. There is always a price for the favours of great men. Come now, tell me! If I am to owe my life to anyone, I want to know the extent of the debt.'

'The debt would be paid,' she thought, but did not say it.

'Tell me,' he urged again.

She knew she must tell him. She owed him that, if she were one day to be his wife. She had told Sir Gavin that they had no secrets from one another, and it was true. She must not begin now: for one day, otherwise, it might come between them and destroy them.

But it was not easy. She bent her head again, and searched for the words.

'He . . . he said he would do all in his power to have you set free if . . .' her voice fell to a near whisper, 'if I would bed with him, as his mistress.'

She felt the hand on her shoulder tighten fiercely, so that she cried out at the pain. She could feel the anger quivering through him and when she looked up she saw a light she had never observed before sparkling in his eyes.

'God damn him to Hell! To breathe a hint of such corruption near your sweet ears—to torment your loving heart with such a choice. No, Honoria, for him there can be no forgiveness, not ever, not for eternity!'

Honoria gazed at him in amazement. This was not the gentle Philip she knew. She had not known him capable of such fury. Gone now was the man who could not bear to hurt his worst enemy, unfailingly kind, always understanding.

Then the anger died as quickly as it had come, though she heard its trembling undercurrent still in his tone. He looked into her eyes with the utmost gravity, and said:

'You are not even to think of it, Honoria. Under no

circumstances. I know that it is only a measure of your love for me that you could even entertain the idea for a moment. But I think you know very well that I do not want my life at that price: it is infinitely too high, my dear. No, Honoria, I would rather suffer the most terrible tortures, endure a death far worse than any I shall have to face, than know that you had endangered your immortal soul to save my skin.'

She had known all along that this would be his reaction; and yet now he had spoken, she felt dismayed, chilled. For what hope was there left?

'Then what are we to do?' she whispered, white to the lips.

He held her lightly in his arms, his face lit with that tranquil smile.

'Pray, my dear. And face whatever comes with faith and courage. It's all we can do. But it is enough.'

Outside, heavy steps approached, and the key grated in the lock.

She returned Philip's gaze with bleak eyes which reflected none of his assurance. He kissed her then and went on, his tone suddenly brisk and practical:

'You must go home, Honoria, at once, as soon as you can. You can do no good lingering here, and Mother needs you at this difficult time. Did you have permission to come to London?' She shook her head. 'That was foolish. It will not help if you find yourself in trouble too. Go home, and stay there. If . . . when I know . . . when it is settled, I shall ask to see you. Then they will send for you. But you are not to come again without permission.' His hands moved to frame her face. 'I know it is hard, Honoria, far worse for you than it is for me. But have courage. And forget that man: don't let the thought of him trouble you. He is beneath contempt. We have no need of his kind.' He kissed her again, as the warder moved impatiently behind him. 'Go home, and take my love to Mother—and be brave.'

She was weeping as the warder touched her arm and led her away. She followed him blindly, stumbling in the dim light along the endless passages, the crashing of that great door echoing in her ears long after they had left it far behind. And his voice, warm and gentle: 'Go home . . . go home.' Home. Alone. Without him. To comfort Aunt Anne for his loss. She could not bear it.

A hand grasped her arm, and she looked round. Through a haze of tears she saw that her companion had halted in a wide well-lit passage by another heavy door. She thought for a moment that they had reached the room where her uncle waited, and then she saw that it was quite a different place. She was sure they had not come this way before.

'What—?' she began in bewilderment.

He signed to her to be quiet, and knocked briskly on the door. Inside a voice answered, and he turned the handle and gestured to her to go in.

'Mistress Somervell, my lord,' he said. 'As you ordered.'

CHAPTER
FIVE

FIVE men sat facing her across a long polished table littered with papers. Their faces were in shadow, for behind them wide windows looked over the river, and threw their shapes into silhouette. Four men had their eyes turned to gaze at her; and a fifth, in the centre, whose head was bent and hand busy with a quill in a large leather-bound book, gave no indication that he knew she was there.

It was worlds removed from the place where Philip was held, this wide room, with its shining floors and panelled walls and exquisitely plastered ceiling. Worlds away, and yet Honoria knew with a relentless and sickening instinct that she was here, now, because of Philip. In the long silence which greeted her entrance, while their eyes took her in and her heart thudded with fear, the only sounds were the crackle of the fire in the wide hearth, the thin whine of the wind outside, and the scratch of the quill on the page. For those horrible long moments Honoria tried to think who they might be, and what they might want with her.

But she knew. She knew even as the man in the centre spoke, in a cool expressionless voice, without pausing or looking up.

'Be seated, Mistress Somervell, and tell us your business here.'

A single chair, carved and uncushioned, faced them across the table. After a moment's hesitation she took her place there and waited, unsure of what he meant.

The man laid aside his quill at last and scattered sand on the page to dry the ink. Not until he had blown it clean did he look up. His eyes were sharp, shrewd, as if they read every thought.

'Well?'

'I . . . I don't know what you mean, sir.'

'"My lord"!' one of the other men corrected her. 'Not "sir", my lord.'

'My lord': she knew now. She should have known before, of course, for there could be no one else so small and hump-backed, with such penetrating eyes, who would order her to be brought before him. Robert Cecil, Earl of Salisbury, Viscount Cranborne, Secretary of State to the King. The implacable enemy of all of her faith. She hoped fervently that the ripple of fear within her had not left its mark upon her face.

'My lord,' she added obediently, though her voice emerged only with difficulty.

'I wish to know your business here,' Salisbury repeated. Even now the impatience was scarcely audible in his tone. He was a patient man, experienced in moving with painstaking, calculating thoroughness towards his goal.

Honoria did not reply at once. Surely they must know what had brought her to the Tower? What kind of game was it they were playing with her? Or was it no game at all, and had Sir Gavin tried to protect her by concealing her visit from the authorities? After all, it had been an unexpected kindness for him to send her the pass. Perhaps he was capable of other acts of kindness too.

'I think you must know that, my lord,' she said at last, cautiously.

'I wish to hear it from your lips, Mistress Somervell.'

So they did know. Not that she had ever really doubted it.

'I came to visit my cousin, Master Philip Blount, my lord. He is held prisoner here. I . . . I had a pass, my lord.'

No flicker of interest showed in the shrewd eyes.

'But you came to London without permission.'

She realised with a shiver that his words were not a question, but a statement. She made no reply, because he clearly expected none.

'Of what did you talk during your visit, Mistress Somervell?' he went on.

She wondered with a sudden flight of fantasy if he had somehow managed to hide his spies in the walls of Philip's cell to overhear every word they had exchanged. But that at least was surely beyond even Salisbury's powers.

'I asked after his health,' she said slowly, 'and gave him news of his mother.' What else could she say, that could be sure to do him no harm?

'Very pretty and domestic,' observed Salisbury, his voice as expressionless as ever. He watched her in silence for a moment through narrowed eyes, then leant forward suddenly, his tone sharpened, alert.

'What do you remember of Master Robert Catesby's visit to your house at Lower Kilworth in September of this year, Mistress Somervell?'

The unexpectedness of the question made her gasp. It was a moment or two before she had collected her wits sufficiently to wonder what to say. Should she deny the visit altogether? Or describe it as a simple domestic occasion, of no interest or significance? She remembered Philip's preoccupied look after Catesby had left that day, and his words just now: 'I told them the truth.' If the truth would do him harm, then it had already been done. She could not make it worse, unless she tried to conceal the facts and showed instead how very significant she thought the whole incident had been. And so, praying silently that Philip would not suffer any more for her words, she told them everything as she remembered it.

As she spoke Salisbury remained leaning forward, listening intently. At his side, a secretary made notes.

The other men were silent, attentive, making no comment, showing no emotion.

Afterwards, they gave no indication that her story had confirmed Philip's words; in fact made no comment at all. She had no means of knowing whether she had helped or hindered his case, or whether perhaps her statement had made no difference.

'Now I want to know what explanation Master Blount gave you of that visit,' Salisbury continued smoothly, when she paused at last.

'How do you know he gave me any explanation?' she returned, in a small gesture of defiance.

'It would seem likely. You are betrothed, soon to be married. You have always been close.'

Did he know everything there was to know about her? Had she been followed everywhere, had the servants been endlessly questioned? She remembered the pock-marked man she had seen in the street this morning. Had she been right about him?

Or had one man only done all Salisbury's work for him? One man in whom she had confided freely before she knew what he was, who knew of her visit to the Tower because he had sent her the pass—one man who had every reason, as he saw it, to wish to be revenged upon her.

With a sinking heart and growing despair she told them all that Philip had said to her just now in his cell, all the harmless-seeming details which would be enough to condemn him to death. And all the time she remembered that if they had the story from him they did not need her evidence; and wondered why, then, they had summoned her here.

They asked her next about Philip's visit to Flanders, and she wished feverishly that she knew exactly how much he had told them about it. But they gave no indication, and again she had to tell them the truth, simply, carefully, without embellishments. If only she could be sure she was not tightening the noose about him with every word she spoke!

And then they began to question her about herself: her dead parents, her aunt, her friends, the few visits she made in the neighbourhood of her home, her thoughts about the government and its treatment of the Catholics, her dealings—if any—with the Jesuits, her religious beliefs. Incessantly, following in swift succession, one after the other, the questions came. Apparently unrelated, insignificant, but always probing and relentless, always demanding an answer. And not once did they let her know why they questioned her, or what they hoped to learn.

It seemed at last as if she had been there for hours on that hard chair facing her inquisitors. She felt lost and alone and very frightened. And utterly bewildered, unable to think clearly, to concentrate on the answers she gave. Sometimes she thought they repeated a question, asked and answered long since, as if they hoped to trap her into a different response. But by then she could no longer remember any reply she had given.

When in the end a long silence followed her final answer she felt utterly weary. Through her exhaustion she heard Salisbury speak, heard them summon a guard, and realised she was being dismissed. She was almost ready to weep with relief, but she bit her lip. Rising to her feet she said as steadily as she could:

'I may go now?'

'From this room,' said Salisbury. 'Not from the Tower.'

She sank back onto the chair, white to the lips.

'Why? Why . . .? My lord, what have I done?'

She never knew what his answer would have been, for at that moment a man came with a letter—an urgent letter, he said—and handed it to the Secretary of State.

Salisbury opened it calmly, and ran his eyes quickly over the contents. She saw the little frown gather on his brow, saw him exclaim silently beneath his breath. Then he handed the letter to his neighbour to read, and turned to Honoria.

'You may go,' he said. The irritation in his tone was unmistakable.

It was not until the guard brought her at last to a small room, and she saw her uncle sitting there, almost beside himself with anxiety, that Honoria realised she had reached the gatehouse. They had let her go.

As soon as Honoria crossed the threshold of her uncle's house the inevitable reaction set in. Until that moment she had been numbed, dazed by all that had happened, allowing William Somervell to lead her in silence from the Tower to the waiting coach, sitting motionless at his side until they came to a halt before his front door, stepping obediently down to the street and then following him up the steps and into the hall. And then she sank down at the foot of the stairs and all her long-suppressed emotions gave way at last, her fear and grief and confusion and misery, pouring out in an uncontrollable flood of tears.

William Somervell stood over her in consternation, murmuring soothing words with total lack of effect, Jane Porter brought wine and tried to rouse her with affectionate scolding. But still Honoria lay on the stairs, her face hidden against her outstretched arms, shaking with dreadful sobs, heedless of all they could do or say to comfort her.

She wept on, oblivious of the hammering on the door, the rush of feet to answer it, the exclamations of astonishment, wonder, dismay: oblivious of everything until a sudden awed and ominous silence penetrated her distress, and she raised her head slowly, to meet the bright, amused gaze of Sir Gavin Hamilton.

He stood over her, tall, arrogant, magnificently dressed, in total contrast to the sombre misery of her mood and of the scenes in which she had played a part today at the Tower. Behind him Jane and William Somervell hovered anxiously, embarrassed and unsure of themselves. Sir Gavin bowed and held out his hand.

'Let me assist you to rise, Mistress Somervell,' he said amiably, his matter-of-fact tone ignoring her prostrate position, her tear-stained face.

She gulped back her tears and pulled out a handkerchief, blowing her nose vigorously.

'I do not need your help, sir,' she said coldly, when she had regained sufficient control over her voice. She reached for the newel post and pulled herself to her feet. Her knees felt weak, and she was unbearably weary. She wanted most of all to be alone, and quiet, and to rest. But she would not let him see it.

'Sir Gavin does us the honour of calling to enquire after you, and after young Philip,' her uncle broke in, aware of the need for some explanation. He sensed that she would blame him for admitting so exalted a guest to witness her grief, but Sir Gavin had allowed him no time to protest before he was in the house.

Honoria stood clinging to the newel post and gathering her thoughts together. The blue eyes watching her were full of amusement still, and she coloured slightly. How dared he come now, to gloat over her unhappiness, when if he had any feelings at all he must guess what she was suffering! And did he know all she had gone through today? Did he know that Salisbury had questioned her? Did he know that she had very nearly been held in the Tower, a prisoner as helpless as Philip, and with less reason? He had sent her the pass: had he planned the rest as well? She wished she had some means of finding out, but she would not ask him. To do so would demonstrate more surely than ever how shaken she was, how unhappy. And she wanted, moreover, to take her leave of him with dignity and retire to her room.

'I must thank you, sir,' she said with icy courtesy, 'for assisting me to visit my cousin. And now I must bid you good-day.'

He smiled with careless charm.

'Not so fast, Mistress Somervell. Surely you owe me something warmer than such very scant thanks.' He turned to her uncle. 'Master Somervell, you have I am sure a parlour where your niece and I may talk alone for a little while.'

'No!' exclaimed Honoria sharply. He turned to look at her with raised eyebrows, and she went on more calmly: 'Sir, you and I can have nothing to say to one another. I must ask you to leave.'

She caught sight of her uncle's appalled face, ludicrously dismayed at such churlish treatment of so important a personage, but she saw it without sympathy. He did not know Sir Gavin as she did, to her cost.

But Sir Gavin was not so easily deflected from his purpose. Before she knew what was happening he had linked her arm through his and turned again to her uncle.

'We may make use of this room?' His free hand gestured towards the parlour door, and she saw her uncle bowing his effusive agreement. 'Good. Then I should be grateful for some refreshment; and I don't doubt that your niece also would be glad of something to revive her a little.'

Not in your company! thought Honoria angrily. She longed to pull her arm from his grasp, to drag herself free and make her escape. But his hold on her was too firm, and she would not stoop to an unseemly struggle.

So she found herself very soon seated at the fireside in the parlour while he stood with his back to the flames and gazed at her. His expression was unfathomable, but at least that detestable amused glint had gone. She closed her lips firmly, raised her head, and carefully avoided his eyes.

He poured her uncle's best wine into two glasses and handed one to her. When she would not make a move to take it he placed it without a word on a table at her side. Then he said:

'I trust you found your cousin well, and in good heart?'

Her eyes flashed furiously at him, and he gave a faint smile.

'As well as could be expected, in the circumstances,' he answered for her. 'I imagine your visit only served to confirm what I had already told you: that without my help he will die.'

'Is that why you arranged it?' she demanded. He considered for a moment.

'Yes, you could say it was.' He took one of Jane Porter's delicate saffron cakes from the plate where the housekeeper had placed them, and bit into it reflectively. 'I wish you would take some refreshment, Mistress Somervell,' he said easily. 'You look as though you stand in need of it.'

She could feel the dried tears stiff on her face, the wisps of hair falling loose about her forehead, and she could well imagine that her appearance was anything but dignified, but she would not allow him to see that she was aware of it. She ignored his observation, and said, her eyes challenging him:

'You knew of course that I was taken for questioning before the Earl of Salisbury whilst at the Tower?'

She saw no flicker of surprise in his eyes, nor any other emotion. He was silent for a moment, and then answered her question with another, smoothly put:

'What do you think, Mistress Somervell?'

She felt a little quiver of anger that he should play with her so.

'I think,' she said sharply, 'that you are quite capable of having arranged it all.'

He smiled, not very pleasantly, and gave a slight bow.

'You have gauged my character with consummate accuracy, Mistress Somervell: and the extent of my influence. I am also, of course, quite capable of having you released from so unpleasant a predicament as that in which you found yourself today.'

She coloured slightly, her anger mounting. What was he implying? That he had indeed caused her to be taken for questioning? That he had, on the contrary, arranged for her release? Or that he had been responsible for both events? Even that, she knew instinctively, was possible.

'But how were you to know that I was in that predicament if you had not arranged it?' she asked pointedly.

'I have friends and informants wherever I might happen to need them,' he said blandly.

She remembered the man with the pock-marked face, and wondered. How many others had there been since she came to London, watching her every move, reporting everything to him? Did she owe all that had happened today to this man, or had Salisbury, too, played his own part? She shivered, and began to understand how a fly might feel, defenceless against the clinging, enveloping meshes of the spider. Scarcely knowing she did so she took the glass from the table beside her, and sipped a little of the wine. Then she raised her eyes to his face and asked, trying to sound as if she did not mind what his reply should be:

'Do you intend to tell me what part you played?'

He smiled, as if he enjoyed her discomforture.

'Perhaps.' He gazed at her for a moment or two, his eyes holding hers in silence. Then he said: 'I will relent, Mistress Somervell. I played some part, but it was not all in my hands. It was Salisbury who chose to have you questioned: it was I who sent word, with the King's authority, to have you released.'

'So,' she retorted sharply, 'I suppose I must thank you that I am not there still.' There was not the remotest hint of gratitude in her tone. She spoke as if she hated him for it.

'As you choose, Mistress Somervell. But as you doubtless suspect, I was not without ulterior motives. I do nothing which does not suit my purpose. Simple good nature is not my style.'

'I know that well enough!' she exclaimed with feeling. 'What did you expect then? That I would throw myself upon you in a passion of gratitude?'

He grinned suddenly, with an unexpectedly boyish charm.

'One can always hope.' Then the smile faded. 'But no, mistress. For one thing it is a little difficult to bed a prisoner in the Tower—' He saw the blush flood her face and continued smoothly: 'But chiefly I hoped you would draw certain lessons from my actions today. In part, from your meeting with your cousin, face to face with the danger in which he stands. And also from the speed with which you were released when my message came.'

She digested this for a moment, and then said bitterly:

'Oh yes, I can draw the lessons well enough. That Philip's danger is real and immediate, and that your power is limitless, should you choose to exercise it.'

'You are an apt pupil, Mistress Honoria,' he commented. 'But there is another lesson, too, which you could take to heart: that it is not your cousin only who is in danger. You are Philip's near relation, and his betrothed. If he confided in anyone, he would confide in you. Might not you also be implicated in his treason, if he is found guilty? I think that is how Salisbury looks upon you.'

She shivered, and took another sip of the wine. She had not eaten since breakfast time—and scarcely then—and now she began to feel a little light-headed. But it strengthened her courage.

'My conscience is clear,' she said defiantly.

'So, I suppose, is your precious Philip's. But that will

only serve to give him courage on the scaffold.' He saw her whiten, and came nearer, to stand looking down at her, smiling slightly. 'But let's try to put these unpleasant thoughts behind us, sweeting. You know, don't you, how you may secure your cousin's release, and your safety? It is in your hands.'

She rose to her feet, her colour rising.

'Never!' she cried. But he was closer now that she was standing, disturbingly near, his eyes intent upon her face. She cursed the frantic beating of her heart, the quickened breathing, the dizzying awareness of how blue his eyes were, how powerful his presence. She tried to sit down again, but his arms were about her, holding her, drawing her nearer. She fought a desperate battle with herself, against the magnetism of his presence, against the force that was sapping her strength, battering down her defences, destroying inexorably every particle of her will power. And then she knew the battle was lost, as his mouth found hers and she felt her arms reach out to clasp him, and she yielded, all resistance gone, to the unutterable sweetness of his embrace. She had lost, but she hated herself for her weakness, and him most of all for playing upon it. Yet even then, when he released her at last, it was all she could do not to cry out in dismay.

He held her at a little distance and looked down at her, smiling with obvious satisfaction, hatefully aware of his power over her.

'Why not give in, sweeting?' he asked softly. 'It is what you want. What could be easier, than to follow your inclinations and save your cousin's life?'

'Easier, perhaps,' she retorted sharply, 'but not therefore right.'

With an enormous effort she pulled free of his arms, and retreated behind her chair, trembling but defiant.

'Have no doubt, sir,' she said clearly, 'that whatever power you have over me, and over those I love, I shall never freely, of my own choice, give you what you ask.

Not to save Philip's life, nor mine, shall I yield to your foul desires. You are wasting your time here, and mine.' She moved towards the door, and turned as she reached it to say: 'I do not wish ever to see you again.'

And then she left him.

How like a woman, he thought ruefully, to succeed always in having the last word! But she had not done so, after all, for he had not finished with her yet. No woman had ever defeated him, and she would not be the first to do so. He would call again tomorrow, and the day after, and the day after that, for as long as was necessary until at last she gave him what he asked. What happened to Philip Blount he did not care: he was only a useful tool. But somehow, by whatever means, he would make Honoria come to him, on his terms, in his way.

He went with arrogant dignity to take his leave of William Somervell.

CHAPTER
SIX

'I NEED to have my friends about me,' said the King,
laying a confiding hand upon Sir Gavin's arm.

He had summoned his favourite to him early in the
morning. A small part of his affection for Gavin sprang
from something quite other than the younger man's
obvious physical attractions. Like the King himself, Sir
Gavin had suffered a bitter and lonely childhood, and
struggled through poverty and hardship to his present
heights. Though for Gavin, the child of the streets, there
had not even been the doubtful compensation of rank.
That past had left its mark on both of them, and brought
them closer now.

Since the events of November 5th the King had turned
more than ever to the support of his Scottish favourites.
Not that the Scots had proved in the past any more
trustworthy than the English, but at least he knew where
he stood with them.

This morning he had passed a pleasant hour or two in
Sir Gavin's company, deep in agreeable conversation
and argument. Sir Gavin was tactful enough to let him
have the better of the talk, every time. It had proved
infinitely soothing to his troubled nerves.

Now Sir Gavin linked his arm through the King's, and
bent closer.

'Your rare qualities, sire, will always assure you of
loyal and loving servants,' he murmured in the royal ear.

Secretly he was wishing that the King would dismiss
him, and set him free to call on Honoria. Had she
regretted her rejection of him last night? That she was

attracted to him he knew. All he needed was time, and she would be his . . .

He realised abruptly that the King was speaking again.

' . . . She came to court but yesterday, my Gavin,' he concluded, as Gavin retrieved his wandering attention.

'Yes, sire,' said Gavin blankly, though he hoped that his smooth tones concealed the fact that he had missed most of the King's words. Not for nothing was King James's wisdom praised, for all that most of the talk was flattery. Now he looked shrewdly up at his favourite.

'I was saying, my Gavin, that she would be a good match for you. I spoke of the Lady Philomena Sidney: but newly widowed, of the best blood, and possessed of a fortune. You would have my blessing for the match.'

For a moment surprise deprived Sir Gavin of his poise. He had taken it for granted that one day he would marry, as advantageously as possible, but he had not expected to be faced with the prospect so soon, and at the King's instigation. He tried to remember all he could of Lady Philomena Sidney—there had been much talk when her husband died, for she was an enticing prospect as a consequence.

'She was connected by marriage with the Sidneys, of course,' said Sir Gavin reflectively, 'but is she not also, sire, some connection of my lord of Salisbury?'

'Indeed, my Gavin. And also sprung of some of the oldest noble blood in England. For you—' He looked up, his expression full of meaning.

Yes, thought Sir Gavin, for me, the outsider, to be allied with the most powerful families in the land: it is exactly what I need to make my position sure. His eyes gleamed at the prospect.

'I should like very much to meet the lady, sire,' he said.

The King smiled and patted his hand.

'And so you shall. She is here today. Let us go at once

and make you known to her.'

Sir Gavin found himself led from the King's small private chamber to the hall beyond where courtiers waited their turn, or paid their attentions to the ladies. Lady Philomena, as befitted her widowed state, sat a little apart in a far window, but a throng of men had followed her there. Sir Gavin felt sure, seeing her, that he would have guessed who she was without the King's word in his ear.

Tall, pale, long-nosed, with prominent teeth and a haughty expression, she sat unmoved by the compliments paid her by attentive courtiers. Somehow, in her black widow's gown and severe headdress she was like a strange caricature of Honoria: Honoria without her alluring beauty, without the passionate depths beneath the cool exterior. Lady Philomena, Sir Gavin felt sure, was cold to the very core. But in a wife that did not matter very much. What was important was the wealth and prestige she had to offer. That made the lady a hundred times more appealing than the beautiful Mistress Somervell.

He conjured up his most charming smile and set out to melt a little of the ice.

It was hard work, but his own attractions and the King's clear approval had begun to move her a little by the time he took his leave of her and set out for home.

He felt exhilarated now. If he had to marry, then he had found the ideal bride. She would not hamper his freedom, for she was well accustomed, he knew, to the ways of an errant husband. She would not interfere with his choice of bedfellow, so long as he did his duty by her.

Now, then, at last, for Honoria! Now to see those eyes flash in anger, and then soften, darken with passion, to feel her melt against him, all tremulous desire—

He leapt from his coach and ran into the house with long strides, calling for his man to bring a change of clothes, brushing aside the thin individual with the instantly forgettable face who was waiting in the hall to speak with him.

'Not now, man,' he said. 'John! The tawny velvet—now, at once!'

He was halfway upstairs when the thin man caught up with him and seized his arm. He turned impatiently.

'Not now, Sim! I've better things to do with my time.'

'But, sir, the woman—'

Sir Gavin smiled.

'Ah, I've my own woman, Sim.'

'That's just it, sir. Mistress Somervell—'

Sir Gavin stopped dead, his smile fading.

'Mistress Somervell? What of her?'

Sim was suddenly nervous, shifting from one foot to the other, stammering uncomfortably.

'Well, sir . . . er . . . it's like this . . .'

'Come now, man, what's happened? What of Mistress Somervell?'

'She's . . . she's left, sir.'

'Left? What do you mean?'

'Left London, sir. For the country—'

Sir Gavin's arm swung out and struck him a great blow which sent him spinning halfway down the stairs. He reached out wildly for the banister and clung to it to steady himself, gazing up fearfully at his master, then he retreated step by slow step to the safety of the hall. He was relieved when Sir Gavin showed no sign of following him for the time being.

'Damn you,' said Gavin. 'She can't have done. I spoke with her just last night—'

'Yes, sir,' nodded Sim. 'She left before dawn this morning in her uncle's coach. I saw her go, and the wench at the house said she was on her way home.'

Sim had known Sir Gavin would be angry, but he had not expected quite the thunderous frown which marked his brows, the clenched fist thrust with a crack against the other hand.

'Damn her!' said Sir Gavin, and again: 'Damn her—damn, damn, damn! Why didn't you tell me before?'

'You were not up when I called first, sir. And then you went to Court and would not speak with me.'

'Damn you, too! Get your ugly face out of here and tell them to saddle the grey—now, at once! I want him at the door in two minutes, or there'll be heads broken—run!'

Sim needed no second bidding. Nor did the groom to whom he carried the message. They had the horse saddled and stamping with eagerness at the door by the time Sir Gavin emerged, his court magnificence covered with a heavy dark cloak against the bitter wind.

At a corner of the street, a man with a pock-marked face drew back into a doorway as the horse was led forward.

Sir Gavin flung himself into the saddle, thrusting the groom aside with a kick from his booted foot, and urged the horse into a gallop. On, on at furious speed, heedless of any obstacle, he took the road to the north, the road Honoria must have travelled all those hours ago.

The grey was his latest acquisition, a tall, powerful, spirited creature of unflagging stamina. He tested those qualities now to the full, pressing on at a relentless pace, oblivious of all but the need to find the woman who had dared to defy him. He paused only twice, just long enough to learn that she had passed that way, and that she was not travelling quickly. With luck, he would come up with her before she reached home.

It began to rain, a heavy drenching rain carried on a fierce wind from the north. But he did not notice, riding on against the worst it could do, his face a mask of determination. There was no charm in his expression now, no softness, only a stern rigidity which set his mouth in a harsh line and gave a cruelly brilliant light to his eyes. For this he would punish her, for this he would use her without mercy!

And then the horse stumbled, almost throwing him, and shuddered to a halt. Even the harsh thrust of the spurs failed to increase his pace beyond a painful trot. Sir Gavin gave up the attempt at last to urge him on and dismounted, swearing volubly under his breath. And then he cursed the more, for that valuable tireless horse had cast a shoe.

He stood in the road in the rain gazing in impotent fury at the beast. And it was then at last that he came to his senses.

'What the hell am I doing here?' he said. He looked around. There was no village near, no passer-by in sight. The road was deserted. He stood alone with a disabled horse in a relentless downpour which had already soaked him to the skin despite the cloak, and he had come without servants, without baggage, without money.

And for what? To pursue a stubborn woman who had spurned his advances.

In spite of the rain and the cold he reddened. Thank God no one was about to see him! He, who prided himself on his power and his dignity, had allowed his anger to lead him to the most foolish and pointless of actions. What would he have done when he came up with her? He did not want to take her by force. He wanted her to come humbly, willingly, acknowledging his hold over her. This was no way to achieve that end.

And in any case what woman was worth all this trouble? He smiled ruefully. Other men, after all, met with rejection again and again. He was a fool to take it so hard that it had happened once to him.

Let her go, he thought. I'm well rid of the frigid wench.

Slowly, he turned the horse and led him gently back to the last village he had passed, to find a blacksmith, and the comforting shelter of an inn. Fortunately, his name and his reputation and his magnificent clothes—however drenched—were enough to guarantee him the best attention, even without money. He managed to invent a plausible story to explain his plight.

It was fully dark by the time he rode home at last through the London streets. Even the grey had tired by now. To either side the lighted windows testified to the warmth and comfort of the homely firesides within. Yes, there were other things in life than a cold red-headed bitch who would not acknowledge his charm. A splendid marriage to a complaisant wife of the King's choosing, that was better. And a certain plump blonde who was only too happy to give him all he asked for, whenever he chose.

He demanded a meal and a change of clothes as soon as he reached home, and then set out again to console himself with the willing charms of his mistress.

Yet somehow he did not find quite the consolation he had expected. She was as willing as ever, her room as perfumed and inviting, and the bed with its silken sheets as softly yielding as her body. But despite everything, his thoughts returned to Honoria. That enticing blend of purity and passion . . . those strange unforgettable eyes. . . There was something infinitely intoxicating in them to his jaded palate. Some promise of excitement which the experienced whore in his arms could never offer.

As he rode home in the early morning he felt a sharp quiver of anger. He must have her after all. It was the only way to prevent her from disturbing his peace, and his enjoyment. She was a constant irritation, which he must take and control, and then it would cease to trouble him.

Before he went to bed to sleep off the effects of the night he summoned Sim.

'Go down to Warwickshire, find where she lives. And make certain other discreet enquiries . . .'

Not until he had seen the man on his way was he able at last to rest.

But there was no rest for the man with the pock-marked face: he followed Sim silently, through every twist of the streets.

'Thank God you are safe home!'

As Aunt Anne enveloped her in an emotional embrace, Honoria noticed, with sharp anxiety, that she had aged. These last few short days seemed to have added endless lines of care to her tired face, deepened the shadows about her patient eyes. Philip was right, thought Honoria, I should not have left her.

For what, after all, had she achieved? Nothing, nothing at all but a visit to Philip, and that had only served to make her realise how hopeless was his position. As for her meeting with Sir Gavin: better not to think of that. It had brought her only nights of sleeplessness, days of anxiety and doubt.

'Come in out of this rain,' urged her aunt, and Honoria went with her into the chill darkness of the house. How different it seemed, after the warmth and light of her uncle's house, the fires blazing in every hearth, the brilliance of candles all around. Here the parlour fire was meagre, kept alight but no more, and the solitary candle seemed helpless against the shadows. But perhaps it was fitting, after all, that they should have little more comfort than Philip, in his cheerless cell.

'Now tell me, dear, what has happened? Have you seen Philip? How are things with him? And what of you? I feared you might be in trouble for travelling without permission. They are becoming very strict of late. Many of our friends have been in trouble, one way or another—'

Honoria reassured her. That frightening interview with Salisbury must remain a secret, for her aunt's peace of mind. She had half expected that she would be prevented from returning home today, or even pursued and arrested. Salisbury must have some case against her, to have threatened her with imprisonment, and if not he, then there was one other who might, perhaps, have tried to keep her in London. But she must not think of him.

She gave her full attention, instead, to her aunt, comforting her, as they shared a frugal supper, with the thought of Philip's courage and serenity. It was the only crumb of comfort she could find in all that had happened.

It was far into the night before they ceased talking and went to bed. And yet Honoria knew that she had told her aunt very little of her visit to London. She said that Philip was well, but there was little hope for him, and that she had seen Sir Gavin Hamilton in vain. She mentioned that last point quietly, in passing, and without detail. As if it were almost without importance.

As it was, of course, for it led nowhere. So she told herself as she closed the door of her room, and looked round at the familiar surroundings which now seemed strange, as if she had been away for months.

Yes, she had been right to come home. Aunt Anne needed her. Here she could put all those disturbing memories behind her. A pity, indeed, that she and Sir Gavin had ever met, but it was, thank goodness, over now, a thing of the past.

Why then was there a tiny, almost imperceptible tremor of regret deep within her at the thought that she would never again have to steel herself to confront him?

Angrily, she did her best to suppress that rebellious sensation, and turned her attention instead to her prayers. As Philip had said, it was all they had left.

CHAPTER
SEVEN

SIR Gavin had once again put his informers to good use. He came to call on Lady Philomena Sidney with a silver pomander box set with sapphires carried by a servant before him: a gift for his future bride.

She received him without enthusiasm, but courteously, extending a long white hand for him to kiss as if she were royalty. Gavin noted with displeasure that Sir Lionel Talbot was already at her side: fair, willowy, an aristocrat to the backbone. The fact that he was insipid, penniless, and a younger son probably did not matter a great deal to Lady Philomena. Nor even, perhaps, that he was not the King's candidate for her hand, for he was known to be Salisbury's choice. His expression, watching the approaching magnificence of Sir Gavin, was full of disdain.

But Gavin was careful to let no trace of his feelings show on his face. The beguiling smile was at its most winning, the deep voice all honeyed sweetness.

'Your beauty, my lady,' he said, his eyes taking in her stiff figure, her sombre clothes, 'even under a cloud, as now, your beauty turns our gloomy winter to gentle summer.' He saw her eyebrows rise incredulously. No one, he suspected, had ever called her beautiful before. And he realised that he had gone a little too far. She was not the most intelligent of women, but even she could not think herself beautiful. The expression of her eyes told him that she knew wherein lay her beauty as far as he was concerned.

'I bring a small token of my esteem and admiration,

my lady,' he went on, his tone more insinuating than ever. He gestured to his servant to present the gift.

This time he had succeeded, he saw at once. Her pleasure showed through the haughty veneer, and she came close to smiling. She reached out and took the pomander box, turning it about in her hands, examining the skilful workmanship, the ornate setting of the jewels, inhaling the perfume of the spices within.

'My most favourite colour, sir,' she said, 'and I delight in sweet odours. How did you know?'

'Instinct, my lady,' he lied smoothly. 'How could it be otherwise than that your eyes, blue as a summer sky, should be reflected in those jewels—which yet hold only a faint imitation of their colour.' Even as the words slid from his tongue, other eyes shone in his memory: many-coloured, changing, as indescribable and elusive in their quality as the patterns of light on water. No jewel, he thought, could ever capture the beauty of Honoria's eyes. Then he gave himself a tiny, almost imperceptible shake. Damn the woman, she must have bewitched him to intrude like this at such a time! With an effort, he concentrated his attention once more on the hard blue eyes watching him from the unappealing face before him.

Sir Gavin was not a man ever lost for words. Compliments and flattery came easily to him, and he had a gift—well cultivated—for fitting his conversation admirably to his company. But Lady Philomena tested his skill to the full. The afternoon passed in slow tedium, as he struggled against his own boredom to arouse her interest. Once she was his wife, he thought, he would avoid her company as much as possible: a few minutes of it at a time were almost more than he could stand, even with the reward of her fortune and high birth as the prize. It was at least reassuring that Sir Lionel remained largely silent, and even appeared to fall asleep at one point, though Lady Philomena, talking avidly of a book of sermons she had enjoyed, failed to notice this breach of manners.

And then she surprised him, ending some long exposition which he had scarcely heard, with the words:

'I hear you have been consorting with Papists, sir.'

He hoped that his astonishment was not too evident, as he replied guardedly:

'Indeed, my lady. That is no light accusation, at this time—'

'Quite so,' she acknowledged severely. 'At this time of all times the King's true subjects must show their loyalty. Not all Papists, I would admit, are tarred with the same brush. But these of which I speak—well! Up to their necks in the affair, from what I hear—or *her* neck, perhaps I should have said,' she added, with a note of asperity.

Salisbury, thought Gavin. Salisbury has been watching me. It was a disquieting thought, and yet scarcely surprising. He was not much loved in England, and if Salisbury could implicate him in treason then no Englishman at court would weep over it, nor, for that matter, would his rivals amongst the Scots. Yes, she must have heard of Honoria from Salisbury, for she was distantly related to him.

He pulled himself together and said blandly:

'Ah, I understand you now, my lady. I see how you could have thought . . . No, my lady, never fear for my loyalty. If I consort—as you put it—with the King's enemies, it is only to seek to bring about their downfall.' Which, he thought to himself, was very largely true, in its way.

He was relieved that Lady Philomena seemed to accept his explanation. She was positively good-humoured by the time he took his leave of her.

But his own mood was not so light-hearted. Yes, Honoria, he was thinking, I shall bring about your downfall. If I have to move heaven and earth I shall do it.

I want my revenge now, more than ever. Revenge for your coming into my life that day and destroying my peace of mind, revenge for your rejection of me, revenge for that humiliating moment in the rain with the shoeless horse, revenge for the doubts Lady Philomena had about me, because of you. Now that Sim has put the means in my hands—Yes, Honoria, you shall fall, very soon!

'This has been the longest winter I can ever remember,' said Anne Blount wearily, as Honoria lit the single candle. It was almost completely dark, and the white shift she was mending had faded to a dim grey blur, but until now she had struggled on as best she could without light.

'It's only just December, aunt,' she said gently. 'Two weeks still to Christmas. There is a great deal of the winter to come.'

The fragile flame caught the gleam of a tear falling slowly down Anne Blount's old cheek, though she quickly brushed it away.

'Sometimes I think it will never be spring again,' she said brokenly, and Honoria knew she was not simply referring to the seasons or the weather. As always these days their thoughts turned to Philip. If only, Honoria thought, there was some news, however slight. Even bad news would almost have been better than this endless waiting, not knowing what was happening, or if he were well.

'Perhaps no news is good news,' she said consolingly, though she did not believe it. She tried not to think of the daily interrogations taking place in the Tower, the torture, perhaps, the many means used to wring confessions from the prisoners, so that they could be brought to trial. No, the absence of news was no comfort at all. For men who plotted to kill their King the eventual trial and condemnation were certain. Only the time was in doubt. She knew too well that she had turned her back on the one thing which could have saved him. It was as inevitable as the dark days of winter that the news when it came would be bad.

They were silent for a while. Often these days they would sit there saying nothing to each other for long hours together. These silences were terrible, filled with the horror of their thoughts and their fears. But it was hard to think of anything to say to pass the time, without going over and over the dreadful thing that had happened.

At last Honoria laid aside her sewing and went to the window to pull the curtains and shut out the darkness. Outside, the trees bordering the garden swayed in the night wind, black branches bent against a ragged inky sky. For a moment, beneath the trees, Honoria thought she saw something move, a figure caught in a faint gleam of moonlight, briefly appearing as the clouds passed over. She was about to remark on it to her aunt, then thought better of it. She had troubles enough without hearing of something which was probably imaginary—or a prowling animal.

As she closed the curtains and quietly resumed her seat, Anne Blount said:

'It was Sir Gavin Hamilton, was it not, whom you saw in London?' She did not sound remotely interested in the question or its answer. Fortunately she did not see the colour flood Honoria's face as she bent further over her sewing.

'Yes,' said Honoria, rather breathlessly.

'I don't listen to servants' gossip as a rule, as you know,' her aunt went on. Unspoken, Honoria knew, was her hope that she might somehow find a tiny crumb of news in the talk of the kitchen. But she said now: 'I heard them say he's like to wed the Lady Philomena Sidney.'

Honoria raised her head.

'That,' she said with emphasis, 'should suit him very well: pride and wealth and bigotry combined. He should be as miserable as he deserves. I shall never forget how she came here when Father was dying.'

She spoke with uncharacteristic venom, for it was a memory which still, after two years, had power to hurt and anger her.

'Yes,' said her aunt, 'and we came off lightly. The Fulwells have had a great deal to suffer at her hands, with their lands lying between ours and hers. Oh!' she exclaimed suddenly. 'That reminds me—I'd quite forgotten. They say the Fulwells are selling all they have and going to live with her father.'

Honoria's hands fell to her lap and lay still.

'Selling? Oh aunt, they will hate that. They have always been happy there. I remember Sir Henry saying that nothing short of starvation would ever make them sell. Is it as bad as that?'

'Starvation?' her aunt sniffed. 'Persecution more like. It's said there's been pressure put on them, from somewhere on high, and threats, too, I hear. It's easy enough just now to find a way of frightening anyone of our faith, as we know too well.'

And I know best of all, thought Honoria. She added aloud: 'It will break their hearts.'

'Maybe,' said her aunt. 'Yet I can't help thinking there are worse things than to be turned from your home.'

'Yes,' agreed Honoria softly.

That dreadful silence again! She jabbed fiercely at the shift with her needle, and succeeded only in pricking her finger. She gave an exclamation, and put it to her mouth, and tried to think of something to say.

'Aunt, do you think Father Swayne will come at all this year, since—?' She left the sentence unfinished, trying not to remember that by now he should have made his visit, and performed the marriage ceremony, linking her life to Philip's for ever.

'I don't know, dear. I don't know. It's a dangerous time to be moving about. But I can't help wishing he'd come. It would be a comfort.'

'And perhaps he could advise us,' added Honoria. She thought suddenly that his advice might be different from Philip's. Was it possible there was still hope? Then she suppressed the thought almost before it came. No, that way was closed: she must not think of it. She had given her word to Philip.

'I doubt it,' said her aunt sadly, shaking her head.

The silence flooded once more into the room and enveloped them.

In the morning, at last, the sun shone. It seemed as if for weeks the heavy greyness of the skies had reflected their own gloom. Now the sunshine seemed to offer some kind of aid to their courage.

'I think I shall ride this morning,' said Honoria at breakfast. 'I shall call on the Fulwells before they leave.'

The air was crisp and clear, though very cold, and Honoria took the long way round to the Fulwells' house at Silston, enjoying the fresh air after being shut up so long in that sad house. She did not mind the slowness of the ambling brown horse she rode: it was good to have time to feast her eyes on the things she had missed so much in London, the delicate tracery of the winter trees against the blue sky, the ruby brilliance of the berries on the hawthorns, the fragile silvery feather-softness of the old man's beard in the hedgerows. The peace and solitude brought healing for a little while to her troubled spirit.

She did not see the soft dove-coloured clouds building up swiftly in the western sky behind her, though she urged the horse into a trot as a chill little wind tugged at her cloak. It was not until the first flakes began to fall, thin and hesitant, that she realised that the weather had changed.

She glanced behind her: the clouds were moving across the sky, shutting out the sun, and the snow was falling steadily, faster and faster, settling in silence on the empty fields. She was nearer to Silston here than to her own home: she must hurry, to reach shelter before the snow grew worse.

But she had gone no more than a few yards further when the snow became a whirling, bewildering blur of whiteness, obliterating every shape of tree and hill, every outline, every trace of the road. She knew every path of this home countryside of hers, but in this sudden blizzard she might have been marooned in an unknown desert for all the use that was to her. The familiar landscape had disappeared.

There was no point now in trying to reach Silston. The only sensible thing was to find shelter until the storm had passed, and she could see her way again. She peered into the dazzling chaos for some sign of a building, or a sheltering group of trees.

For a moment the wind spun the snow in a contrary direction, and she glimpsed dark shapes ahead. Horsemen, two at least, dogs, and, beyond, the brick wall of a barn. Then the storm hid them again, and she was alone.

She pressed on. The horse bent his head against the snow, his pace reduced to a dejected plod. He seemed to have lost heart, but she urged him on. They had almost collided with the barn before she realised she had reached it.

She dismounted and led the horse along the length of the blank wall to find an entrance. She came on it at the far side, a dilapidated wooden door, closed half-heartedly against the storm. Something had been placed just inside to wedge it shut. It did not occur to her until later that no one could have closed it so from the outside. Now she saw it simply as an obstacle, and pushed and heaved against it until it moved slowly open.

Thankfully, for she was shivering now with the cold, she led the horse into the dry dark warmth of the barn, and turned to close the door. The voice, speaking suddenly behind her, made her spin round with shock, and a scarcely suppressed scream.

'Mistress Somervell! What an unexpected pleasure!'

Even if it had been totally dark she would have known him: that deep, lightly accented voice was unmistakable, sending its shuddering vibration through her body. As it was a small high window gave a faint light, and showed her the tall figure, the bright hair, even the ironic amusement of his expression.

She was face to face with Sir Gavin Hamilton.

CHAPTER
EIGHT

SHE felt her limbs turn to water, the colour flood her face. Thank goodness it was too dark for that to be obvious to him, or to those other watching eyes!

For he was not alone: she saw that almost at once. In fact the barn seemed crowded with men in Sir Gavin's green and scarlet livery, as well as horses and dogs, even a hawk she realised, for a man behind him held one perched on his gloved hand.

Instantly, the snowstorm outside seemed less dangerous than the sheltering barn. She turned quickly to the door. As quickly, Sir Gavin slid past her, to stand between her and escape. He smiled slightly, his eyes acknowledging his triumph.

'Have no fear,' he said, 'the door is securely closed. The storm will not reach us here.' He held out a hand, with the graceful courtier's gesture she remembered so well. 'Come and let me find you a seat—I can recommend the comforts of the hay, as a place of repose.'

She ignored the proffered hand, and pulled her cloak more closely about her.

'I shall remain here, sir,' she said, 'with my horse.'

'As you please, mistress,' he replied smoothly, with no trace of annoyance. But he remained where he was, disturbingly close to her.

She felt very vulnerable, standing alone in the dimness with this man she hated, under the curious gaze of his servants. Instinctively, her hand slid into her pocket and fingered the little knife, sheathed in fine leather, which she kept there. She carried it because, from time to time, it came in useful to remove a stone from a horse's hoof, or to perform some task about house or garden. Now it was reassuring to feel it beneath her hand. It was her only protection, if the man at her side should threaten her.

For the moment, though, he made no move to alarm her more than he had already by being there.

And why, she thought suddenly, was he there? Had he followed her even here, to her home, to pursue her to the bitter end? Was there nowhere she could be safe from him? Did that, then, explain the figure she thought she had seen in the trees last night? Was she being watched still?

Then she remembered the Lady Philomena, and relief flooded her, although under it lay another, quite different emotion, which she did not analyse. She felt calmer now, for he was not likely, surely, to endanger his courtship of that eligible widow by making advances to her near neighbour? She raised her eyes to his face, and said lightly:

'I suppose it is the Lady Philomena Sidney who brings you to these parts?'

He raised an eyebrow, and she had a faint impression that he was displeased, but he said only:

'Ah, you know of that?'

'Yes,' she said. Her tone was cool, giving nothing away, but something in it led him to ask:

'Do you mind?'

That startled her from her momentary composure.

'Mind!' she exclaimed. 'I should think not! In fact,' she went on sharply, 'it seems to me to be an eminently suitable match. You deserve each other.'

She rejoiced to see him colour at that, and knew she had stung his vanity. It was a moment or two before he had his temper under control.

'You are acquainted with the lady?' he asked then.

'Yes,' she said. 'Not well, but well enough.'

Her tone was level and unemotional, but he was intrigued by the light in her eyes, like cold fire.

'You do not like her,' he observed.

'I do not know her,' she returned guardedly. 'We met only once at close quarters.'

'Yet your eyes flash when you speak of her. That interests me.'

'It is not my business to tell you the character of your future wife. You will find that out for yourself soon enough. I expect in any case it will be to your taste.'

'Do you suppose it would matter if it were not?' he demanded, smiling slightly. 'I am not courting her for her amiable character.'

'You surprise me!' she said with heavy sarcasm. She turned away from him to peer through a crack in the door. 'I wonder if the snow has stopped.' The white blur visible beyond the door answered her before he spoke again.

'Don't try and change the subject.' He grasped her shoulder and swung her round to face him. 'Tell me why you hate her so.'

At his touch that shameful, all too familiar vibration quivered through her, from the roots of her hair to her fingertips, flooding her face with colour, drawing the strength from her limbs. She said angrily:

'It is no business of yours! Take your hand from my shoulder!'

Smiling impudently, he obeyed. But instead he touched her cheek, lightly, then his hand slid swiftly to her waist, drawing her nearer.

Not again! she thought, as her rebellious body trembled with delight, responding to his lightest touch with helpless desire. With a great effort of will she pulled herself free and retreated as far as she could, to lean against the wall of the barn. This time, for the moment, she was free, but if he chose to come after her . . . There was no escape in here, in the end. She fingered the knife again, her eyes wide, watching him guardedly.

He laughed softly.

'I shall enjoy having you as a neighbour. I hope we shall meet often.'

She shivered, though scarcely with fear.

'Perhaps the Lady Philomena will not have you, after all,' she said. 'She is something of a Puritan.'

'Ah, but we shall be neighbours all the same. Did you not know?'

Surprise stilled her.

'Know what?'

'I have bought Silston, Mistress Somervell. Our land runs together, yours and mine.'

He saw the colour leave her face, and all the warmth of a few moments before. Her eyes were dark with dismay and anger and something uncomfortably close to disgust.

'So it is *you* the Fulwells have to thank for losing all they have! I might have known! Though I can't think I would have believed even you capable of quite that cruelty—'

'Oh, come now, Mistress Somervell!' he exclaimed. 'I have simply bought Silston from its previous owners. That is not a crime.'

'No, persecuting Catholics is not a crime,' conceded Honoria bitterly. 'We know that well enough. So you can do things to us that the law would not allow any other English man or woman to suffer. But don't try to make me believe you bought Silston openly and legally, as you would any other land. I know the Fulwells would never have sold if they were not forced to do so.'

'Ah, but I wanted Silston very much, Mistress Somervell. And when I want something very much, I take it, whatever unpleasantness I may have to face in the process.'

She coloured, recognising what he implied. He

wanted her too, wanted her to submit herself to his will and his demands. But there was only scorn in her tone as she answered:

'Do you sleep easy at nights, Sir Gavin, knowing what you have done?'

He smiled unpleasantly.

'Very easy,' he said, 'for my bed is soft and my roof is sound and my house is warm, and the world is at my feet. Have you not learnt by now that you cannot survive unless you put yourself first and fight all the way for what you want? No one else will look after you, Mistress Somervell, if you do not. I learned that long ago, when my mother kicked me out at five years old to pick a living in the streets. A child is a burden to a whore, you know, mistress. Every day of my life since has only reinforced the lesson I learned then. If I hadn't learned it well, I'd not be where I am now. Not many back-street bastards find their way to the King's favour.'

She gazed at him in silence for a moment, taking in what he said, then asked quietly:

'And are you happy, Sir Gavin? Are you as rich in love and friendship as you are in power and gold?'

'Of course I'm happy,' he asserted. 'I have all I want. As for love, I have every woman I want, save one—'

'That's not what I meant by love,' she retorted, ignoring the implications of what he said.

'It's the only kind I will admit into my life,' he said. 'Love and friendship: two fine words indeed. But if you let emotion take hold of you, you are lost. If you want to succeed, to survive even, then you must have no time for emotion or sentiment or friendship. Then no one can hurt you, or claim to have a hold on you. Friendship is for fools—like yourself, sweet Mistress Somervell. Was not that man Robert Catesby your friend?'

'I would call him so still,' she replied with dignity. 'Even in death I am proud to own him so.'

'Then that proves what I say. For if he had not been a

friend your Philip would not be in the Tower, nor you in this plight.'

'Because you have no friends does not mean you have no enemies,' she said. 'What will you do if your enemies bring you down? Who will care for you then?'

'It won't happen,' he returned. 'I will not allow it to happen.'

There was an expression in her eyes now which he could not read. They rested on his face for a long time before she said, very gently:

'I pity you.'

He drew in his breath sharply, his eyes wide. Pity! He could scarcely believe his ears. Hatred he could understand, or an awed acknowledgement of his power, or anger, even scorn. But pity!

His eyes took in her worn cloak, her threadbare gown, her bare hands reddened with hard work and cold. He was aware of his own contrasting splendour: the furred velvet of his cloak, the rich warmth of his doublet, the fine boots and gloves, the retainers at his command, the dogs and horses—

'Pity!' he exclaimed in utter amazement. 'For what?'

'Because,' she said, 'even if you keep your hold over the King for years and years, one day you will be old, and no use to anyone any more. And when that day comes no amount of wealth is going to stop you from being ill or lonely or unwanted. And then there will be no one to care for you, except the servants who do it because you pay them; and no one to love you—'

'Ah, but Mistress Somervell,' he broke in, 'you too will be old one day, and you may be just as ill and just as lonely and you will have no wealth to cushion you against the harshness of age.'

'Perhaps not, but I shall have memories to warm me, thoughts of those I have loved, who have loved me, and a clear conscience—or fairly clear, at least—and a hope of something better after death.'

He had a sudden overwhelming urge then to take her in his arms and carry her to a shadowed corner of the barn and have his way with her, knowing she would yield however strong her conscience, and so to wipe out that quiet confidence in her eyes, to destroy her peace of mind and force her to face the future with remorse. But he knew instinctively that it would not work, that his triumph would be a very little thing, soon overturned by her repentance and faith and her courage. He had never felt so powerless as he did at this moment, faced with her quiet assurance. Until now he had never felt that little tremor of fear for himself, and for his own future. He searched his mind for the most hurtful words he could find.

'Will your conscience be so quiet when Philip is torn to pieces on the gallows, and you remember you could have saved him?' he asked savagely.

She went white as the snow outside, but still she held her head defiantly.

'Yes . . .' she whispered, but almost as if she were trying to convince herself. 'Yes . . .' Then she went on, in her old firm tones: 'And if I'd given you what you wanted, for Philip's sake, who's to say you'd have raised a finger to help him afterwards? You said yourself just now that self interest is the only thing that rules you. A broken promise must be of no account at all to someone of your kind.'

He smiled ruefully.

'There you have me, of course. You would have to take your choice, Mistress Somervell. But I did mean to keep that promise—and still do. I lose nothing by it. I am high enough in the King's favour to be beyond Salisbury's reach.'

She shrugged, and turned away from him to peer out again through the crack in the door. A faint blue glimmered above the white, and the light was dazzling.

'It's stopped snowing,' she said. 'I am going.' She

reached down to drag the empty barrel away from the door.

'I shall see you home,' he said, as if she were an honoured guest, and this barn his mansion.

'Indeed you will not,' she returned briskly. 'I am not going home yet, in any case. I am going to Silston, to wish the Fulwells as much happiness as they can hope for now. I don't imagine you will wish to see them face to face, after what you have done to them.'

He gave a soft laugh, and began to say something, which she did not hear, and then changed his mind and went on smoothly:

'I can think of nothing which would give me greater pleasure. Except perhaps to ride at your side.'

'That,' she said sharply, 'would give me no pleasure at all. And I will not insult my friends by arriving in your company. If you will not let me go alone, I shall go home sooner than that.'

He took her hand suddenly and raised it lightly to his lips.

'Far be it from me to deprive your friends of the comfort of your presence. I shall allow you to go alone.' His mouth brushed her fingertips once more, and she shivered, lowering her eyes before his intent gaze. 'Until we meet again, Mistress Somervell,' he ended softly.

Even the tone of his voice, when he speaks like that, she thought, even that makes me tremble with desire. She turned abruptly away from him as he held the door open, and led her horse out into the sparkling sunlit world beyond the barn.

Silston Hall lay silently under its mantle of snow, its rosy brick lit to warmth by the sun. Honoria reined in her horse on a little hill not far away, and gazed at it: the Fulwells' beloved home, where she had spent many happy hours in childhood, and since— the place they loved above all others, and must leave, because the King's favourite had cast greedy eyes upon it.

She felt a renewed tremor of anger at the man who would come to live here soon. That momentary pity which she had felt as he spoke, pity for a man who must have endured a great deal from life to fear love so very much; that feeling had gone now, completely. It was the Fulwells she pitied now, with the warm sympathy of a friend who had also suffered at the hands of this ruthless man. She urged her horse forward, down the slope towards the quiet house.

There was no one about outside, though there were fresh tracks of horses in the snow, passing round the back of the house to the stables. Perhaps they had hired wagons to take the possessions they still owned to their new home. But when she reached the stables there was no sign of any vehicle. And there were more horses in the stalls than she could remember having seen before, even in the days of their greatest prosperity. Perhaps other friends had come too, to take their leave. But she thought it a little odd.

She found an empty stall at last for her own mount, and tethered him there, then made her way to the side door by which she generally entered the house when visiting Silston. She had never stood on ceremony with these old friends.

The passage past dairy and kitchen was empty, and the hangings and furnishings—as threadbare as any at Lower Kilworth—had already been removed from the hall, when she reached it. The sun shone on empty boards, and walls marked by odd rectangles where pictures and tapestries had hung. Her footsteps echoed loudly about the room. The silence kept her from calling out, for she feared suddenly that there was no one left to answer. Had they gone already, while she was too wrapped up in her fears for Philip to have time for news of them? But whose then were the horses in the stables?

Beyond the hall the parlour door stood slightly open, and a faint crackling sound caught her ear. There must be a fire in there, for the flickering rosy gold of its light was reflected faintly on the walls inside the door. She knew instinctively that someone sat by that fire.

She drew a quick breath with relief, and crossed the hall, pushing open the door, her voice warm and full of understanding:

'I have just heard the news. I had to come—' And then she stood transfixed.

At the fireside, stockinged feet stretched to the blaze, head turned to look at her round the carved back of his chair, sat Sir Gavin Hamilton. His eyes were very blue, and brimful of amusement.

'You!' she breathed. She felt dizzy, bewildered, quite unable to understand.

Slowly he rose to his feet, smiling broadly.

'You see I am already conversant with the lanes about here: I know the short cuts. I thought I would be here before you.'

'But . . . but . . .' The words she wanted would not come.

'Where are your friends, the Fulwells?' he concluded for her. 'They left two days ago. I am staying here to enjoy a little quiet hunting—and visiting—and to see what my new house requires. I intend to furnish it magnificently.'

Honoria found her voice at last.

'Why did you let me come?' she demanded. But it was a foolish question, for she knew the answer already. He came towards her, still smiling.

'Why do you think? I am delighted you are here. You came to visit the owner of Silston: I am not hindering you in your object. You must take some refreshment, and we can enjoy a little talk before you go—'

'No!' she broke in. Tears of anger and grief were close to the surface. Wherever she turned he was there, and she was in his power, and there was no escape. The tears were for the Fulwells, and herself, and all she loved. 'I am going,' she cried. 'And if you have any human feeling left in you at all, for God's sake leave me alone!'

She turned, and reached the door, but he was quicker. As in the barn he interposed himself between her and the door, pushing it closed.

'Now,' he said, in that perilously soft voice, 'I suggest you make yourself comfortable while I pour you some wine.'

Honoria's hand crept to her pocket, and slid the knife from its sheath. When he looked down he saw the sunlight catch the short shining blade, turned towards him.

'If you do not open the door I shall make use of this,' said Honoria, her eyes bright with unshed tears. 'It is small, but it is very sharp.'

He grinned amiably, and remained where he was.

'I am sure it is, Mistress Somervell. Do your worst!'

Disbelief was clear in his eyes.

In a sudden blaze of fury, Honoria flung herself forward, the blade darting towards the golden velvet expanse of his chest. Just in time he swung his right arm across to catch the knife in the slashed sleeve of his doublet, where it bit deeply and lingered a moment before Honoria drew back and stood gazing at him, breathing hard, the weapon at her side.

He was silent for some time, watching her with an odd crooked half-smile, and something like rueful admiration in his eyes.

'I did not think you meant it,' he admitted.

'Now you know,' she said, unrelenting. 'I shall use it again, to more effect, if you do not let me go.'

'Then you can spare yourself the trouble,' he said lightly. 'I'll not dispute with one so determined—though I could call men enough to overpower you, if I chose,' he added, 'or I could do it myself, knife or no knife.' Her eyes dared him to try, and he opened the door and stood aside.

'You are free to go, Mistress Somervell,' he said, gesturing her past.

Head high, knife still clutched openly in her hand, she moved forward: and slipped, just for a moment, on something underfoot. She looked down briefly, and then gave an exclamation of dismay. His eyes followed hers, from the red stain on the floor to the spreading scarlet on his golden sleeve. And then his gaze met hers, unexpectedly full of consternation.

'I did not know I'd hurt you!' she cried. She dropped the knife and came quickly to his side, all heedless concern. With neat fingers she unbuttoned his sleeve to the elbow, and turned it gently back, exposing the deep gash welling blood to drip upon the floor. He watched her in silent fascination, smiling faintly.

'Have you a clean handkerchief?' she asked, without looking up. He drew one from his pocket and handed it to her: it was of fine linen, lace-edged. She bound it firmly about the wound, and exclaimed again as it grew quickly red.

'You must come and sit down, and raise your arm a little,' she said, her hands curved about the wound, as she turned to lead him to the fireside.

'I thought you wanted to go,' he retorted, without moving. 'Wasn't that the purpose of all this?'

'I didn't mean to hurt you!' she said sharply, and went on in a coaxing tone, 'Come now—'

Still he made no move to obey her.

'Didn't you?' He laughed softly. 'It was a very convincing act of yours, then.'

'Will you stop talking and come and sit down?' she demanded impatiently.

It was his turn now to be bewildered by this sudden transformation in his companion. But he allowed her to lead him back to the chair and there sat down, rather suddenly. All at once he felt overcome with faintness. Honoria noticed his pallor with concern. She dragged a table alongside and placed his arm on it, resting on a cushion; and then turned to the bottle and glasses set at the fireside and poured him some wine.

'Drink this,' she said gently. 'And I'll find something to bind your arm more securely. Is there someone I can call to help?'

'No! . . . No,' he repeated more quietly. Not for anything would he relinquish the soft touch of her hands, the voice warm with concern. In any case the wound might be difficult to explain without embarrassment. He sipped the wine, feeling a little steadier for it, then said: 'You may find what you need in the chest by the window. You are free to use anything you want.'

The chest of clothes had come with him from London. Another time Honoria might have paused to exclaim at the magnificence of the garments there, but now she was concerned only with what was serviceable. In the end she extracted a pair of embroidered silk stockings and a fine linen shirt, and set to work to staunch the still flowing blood. Gavin rested his head wearily on the back of his chair, and closed his eyes.

When he opened them again she had finished and was kneeling at his side looking anxiously into his grey face. He smiled slightly, and tried to think of something to say. But before he could speak she had taken his left hand between her palms and held it there, saying earnestly:

'I am sorry, sir, for what I did to you.'

If he had felt stronger he would have laughed.

'Sorry? Oh, Honoria!' And he was the more amused at her puzzled expression. Did she see nothing incongruous in her regret for the one little wrong she had done him, set against all he had done to her? To most people her action would have seemed completely justified.

He closed his fingers about one of her hands, and raised it to his lips. There was something in his expression now, in spite of his weariness, which she had never seen before: something gentle, and warm, and far removed from his customary light-heartedness. Even the touch of his lips felt different, softer, less ruthlessly demanding.

'There are not many like you at Court,' he said. 'Nor anywhere else, I think.'

Stillness held them there, suspended, while time ceased, and the empty manor house and all the enmity between them no longer existed, just for that moment. Even their hearts seemed to stop beating, as if they were held outside themselves, in some other existence.

Then he released her hand, and she rose to her feet, smoothing her skirts, her manner briskly matter of fact, as if nothing out of the ordinary had happened.

'I must go,' she said. 'But first let me send someone to you.'

'No, I want no one,' he said roughly. His expression was sombre and withdrawn.

'But what if you should grow worse?' she asked anxiously.

'Then I'll call for help,' he returned. 'But I shan't.'

She gazed at him doubtfully for a moment. Certainly he had more colour now, and that dreadful ashen tinge had gone.

'I think you should go to bed,' she suggested gently.

That brought a faint smile to lighten his face, and she blushed at what it implied. 'Gladly, if you would come with me,' said his eyes.

'Good day,' she said stiffly. 'I will see myself out.'

As the door closed behind her, all the humour left his face. His brows drew together in a frown, and he rose unsteadily to his feet and groped his way to refill his glass from the tooled leather bottle at the fireside. He emptied the glass in a single movement, and filled it again, then

tucked the bottle under his sound elbow and made his
way back to the chair.

When the renewed dizziness had cleared, he glowered
into the fire.

Damn the woman! She had done more than hurt his
arm today. He began to believe he had not been far
wrong when he thought her some kind of witch, in her
uncanny power over him. He drained the glass once
more, and watched yet another comforting stream of
crimson liquid pour from the bottle into the carved
crystal goblet in his hand.

Today he had almost allowed himself to feel some of
that dangerous emotion he had schooled himself to shut
out, some unaccustomed warmth of feeling towards the
woman who had knelt at his feet to bind the wound she
had made. It was her body he wanted, and nothing else,
he told himself firmly now. Her body and will under his
control, but with no hold over him, no power to move or
hurt him. He must not forget it, lulled by her soft voice
and gentle hands into lowering his guard. That was not
what had brought him to Silston.

He set himself to imagine her in his luxurious bedroom in London, his willing slave, unclothed, trembling
with desire, that fair slender body yielding to his every
demand. The reflection warmed him, and strengthened
his resolve.

CHAPTER
NINE

HONORIA dreamed that night that Sir Gavin lay sick of a
raging fever. She saw him stretched alone on a hard and
narrow bed in that barely-furnished house, the shadows
dark about him, a single candle flame leaping unsteadily
in the snow-laden wind from an open window. She saw
his arm swollen and hideous where she had hurt him,
saw him toss and turn and cry out with pain. She saw
them amputate his arm, the blood spattering the bed and
the floor, saw him lie still and white, heard him with his
dying breath call curses on her for what she had done.
She woke sobbing and shivering to the cold still darkness
of her room, and knew with relief that it was only a
dream.

Or was it? Wounds could fester—even the smallest of
wounds—especially if untended. Strong men had died
before from so slight a cause, suffered from dreadful
fevers and lost precious limbs. What if Sir Gavin had
fainted after she left him, unable to make anyone hear
his call? What if he had lain there all night with the fire
burned out and no one to care for him? It could happen
so easily. She began to believe it was almost bound to
happen. And then his death would be on her conscience:
she would have been responsible for killing a fellow
human being, as surely as if her knife had struck his
heart. Even though he was her most deadly enemy, that
was an unbearable thought.

She sat up, reached for her rosary and began urgently
to pray for him.

'Please God, let him live! Don't let him die because of
me—make him well!'

Her fingers slid over the beads until they grew numb with cold, and she was shivering uncontrollably. She drew the covers close about her and lay down, trying not to think of what she had done today. But try as she might, Sir Gavin haunted even her wakefulness, his blue eyes, his mocking smile, that dreadful pallor, and the blood dripping to the floor.

She lived through the next few days in nightmarish uncertainty. If only she dared send someone to Silston to ask after him, or—even better, but unthinkable—go there herself, but she could not speak of what had happened to anyone. Even Aunt Anne knew only that the Fulwells had not been there. Honoria had said nothing of who had bought the land.

That last piece of news did not reach Lower Kilworth for another week. Honoria was in the kitchen, helping to prepare pies for Christmas, when Tom came back from market one day with Meg, the maid, full of excitement at his side.

'Now we know who's bought Silston,' said Tom gruffly, stamping the snow from his boots. Honoria's heart gave a great lurch, and the pastry flower she was making to decorate the pie took on a grotesque shape.

'Who would that be, then?' asked Cook, her hands busy with the rolling pin.

'Sir Gavin Hamilton,' said Tom, and Honoria's heart seemed to beat out the rhythms of his name in unison. Had they heard any other news of him?

'The King's great favourite,' added Meg impressively. 'And we *saw* him today, riding through the market with all his men. He is *so* handsome, you would not believe it—'

'Handsome is as handsome does,' said Cook primly.

But Honoria scarcely heard her. A great wave of relief swept her, turning her weak-kneed with gratitude and rosy of face. Thank God! He was alive, and well enough to ride out and impress poor silly Meg with his splendour. Oh, thank God! She almost wept with thankfulness that she had not been responsible for his death. She would never, ever, do such a thing again, whatever danger threatened her.

It was only a few days now to Christmas, and Honoria and her aunt intended to do their best, as far as their poverty allowed, to mark the festive season. But they could not enter into the spirit of things as they had in other years, now that Philip was in the Tower, with that dreadful fate hanging over him.

There was another cause for anxiety too. In her fear for Sir Gavin Honoria had forgotten completely the figure she thought she had seen in the darkness the night before the snow storm. Now it was brought forcibly to her mind again. She woke one morning to find that another light layer of snow had fallen in the night, and went to her window to look out on the early freshness of the garden, each tree delicately outlined in silver. And she saw, with a prickle of fear running down her spine, that there were fresh footprints in the snow beneath the trees, less clearly marked than they might have been elsewhere, for the snow was little more than a faint powdering there. But they were distinct enough for all that: large prints, which only a man's well-shod foot could have made. They led from left to right as far as she could see, as if they encircled the house, but within the shadow of the trees.

She wondered at what time the snow had fallen, and if Tom could have had any reason to be out. She must be sensible, for there might be some very simple explanation. She had brought this foolish nervousness back from London with her, and it would be cowardly to give in to it.

But Tom had not been out in the night. Worse still, he had looked out as the snow began to fall, some time around midnight, and thought he saw something move, quickly hidden again, in the trees.

'It's not the first time, neither, Mistress Honoria,' he added. 'It would be three nights ago now I saw a man watching the stables—when I went to bed the beasts down, that would be, just about supper time. He hopped back into the trees when I looked his way, but I saw him all the same. And I'm pretty sure it was the same man I met in the lane Wednesday noon last, as I came back from market. There was someone at the market, too, hanging about near us, but no, he was a weird looking fellow, with light eyes and pock-marks. It wasn't him, that I'm sure. No, the man in the lane passed me without a word or a look, and I would have thought nothing of him if I'd not seen him in the trees that time. But as it was I'd a good mind to ask him what he did there, where we never see strangers from one year's end to the next. Cook and Meg saw nowt of him—not that I told them of what I'd seen at night. It wouldn't do to scare them.'

Honoria listened in shuddering silence, then she said: 'Why did you not tell me, Tom? I ought to have known.'

'Didn't want to scare you either, mistress. There's nowt we can do about it, in any case. But I'd give a good deal to know what he wants with us.'

Honoria shivered.

'So would I,' she said. Who was it this time who had set spies on them? Sir Gavin? Salisbury? Or another whose reasons she could not even guess at? She raised her troubled eyes to his broad brown face. 'Have you any thoughts on that, Tom?'

'None that would help, Mistress Honoria. Only that it's all of a piece with Master Philip's trouble. And I can't see he's going to catch us doing anything we shouldn't, however long he hangs about out there.'

But Tom was wrong in that reassuring prediction. Within twelve hours they knew how very wrong he was.

To Aunt Anne, however, who knew nothing of the

watcher in the shadows, the arrival just after dark of a
cloaked and weary figure, slipping quietly in by the
kitchen door, was a matter for unqualified rejoicing.
Meg led him to the curtained parlour where Honoria sat
with her aunt, and ushered him into the room in silence,
closing the door behind him, as she had done many times
before. The two women at the fireside turned swiftly and
were on their feet in a moment, coming forward to greet
him.

'Father!' exclaimed Anne Blount, softly. 'Oh, we
scarcely dared to hope! I'm so glad!'

She reached out to take his cloak and led him to the
most comfortable chair close to the fire. But Honoria ran
to close a non-existent gap in the curtains, and her eyes
were dark with fear in her white face.

Father Swayne had known them for a long time, and
was a frequent and welcome visitor. But he was not
simply a priest—a dangerous enough person at any
time—but also a Jesuit. It was firmly believed, by every
Protestant Englishman from Salisbury to the meanest
cow herd, that the Jesuits were deeply implicated in the
dreadful plot against their King. They were the hated
and feared missionary priests, who worked in secret to
destroy the whole fabric of English life.

Honoria and her aunt and their servants knew better
than that, but very likely the man outside did not, and if
he had seen Father Swayne arrive—!

Honoria stood by the window pressing her hands
together, and wondering what to do.

'Whatever's wrong with you, Honoria?' asked her
aunt cheerfully. The priest's arrival seemed to have
driven away all the misery of the past weeks. 'Come and
sit down. Meg will be back soon with refreshment for the
good Father.'

'No—no!' whispered Honoria. She turned her eyes to
their guest. 'Father, you must not stay. A man has been
watching the house for days now. Tom's seen him, too.

We didn't tell you, Aunt, so as not to frighten you, but if he saw you come, Father—' She broke off, moving her hands expressively.

Anne Blount had gone pale, all the new happiness driven out of her in a moment, and Father Swayne's dark eyes were grave.

'I watched the house myself, before I approached it,' he said, 'and I am reasonably sure that I was not seen. But I cannot be certain, of course. And you have troubles enough to bear, without my making them worse.' He rose, and looked about for his cloak, but Aunt Anne clasped his arm.

'No, Father. We're not afraid for ourselves, but for you. You will face certain death if they find you. But where will you go if you leave here?'

He smiled slightly.

'There is always somewhere,' he reassured her. 'I shall be safe enough. I think Honoria is right, and I ought to be on my way. Apart from my safety, and yours, there is Philip to be considered. It will not help his case if I am found here.'

Honoria came forward now.

'I didn't mean to drive you away at once, Father,' she said. 'You must eat first. And if you were seen coming here, then they can follow you as easily if you go. If you were not seen, then you can stay a little, with safety. Besides, what could one man do against us all?'

It was Aunt Anne's turn now to be anxious.

'But what if whoever was watching has gone for help, and comes back with soldiers, while you're still here?'

'That would take some time,' said Honoria. 'Several hours, most likely. And if the worst comes to the worst we have our good hiding place.'

Aunt Anne's face cleared with relief.

'Of course,' she said. 'I had not thought of that—' She turned to the priest. 'We don't wish to put you in any danger, Father, but if you would stay a little—rest and eat—and better still, celebrate the Mass for us while you are here, that would be a great comfort. Then we'll make sure you are not followed when you leave. Tom has sharp eyes and a strong arm.'

The bare little room under the eaves, with its tiny window heavily shuttered, was very quiet that night, but for the low tones of the priest and the hushed responses of the small household gathered there behind the locked door. Honoria felt her troubles and fears and anxieties drain away as she knelt on the hard floor, and reflected that, in the end, their suffering was a very small thing: even Philip's, though she prayed earnestly for his safety. And Sir Gavin, who had seemed so menacing and so dangerous, mattered not at all.

There was no one watching from the windows, for they were all present in the little room, but in the frosty stillness of the night every sound would carry for miles. That was how they all heard it at once, as the priest gave the dismissal and they knelt a moment or two longer in prayer: the hooves ringing on the frozen road, the jangle of harness. Some way off yet, but coming quickly, relentlessly, towards the house.

Honoria rose to her feet, her face white. Her aunt's eyes, gazing back at her, held the same realisation and the same fear. Meg gave a muffled scream, quickly suppressed. Father Swayne finished his devotions, and came towards them: only he seemed to be calm.

'I'll go now, at once,' he said.

Honoria shook her head.

'No, Father, there's no time. Bring everything and come with me. The rest of you, get to bed as quickly as you can—give me that candle, Meg. I'll need it for the moment, but we must have no lights. They must think we were all asleep. Hurry now!'

In a moment they had gone, groping their way in the darkness to their beds. The approaching hooves sounded terrifyingly loud now in the stillness, but Honoria knew they still had a little time.

She led Father Swayne down the stairs to the guest bedroom on the floor below. Its most striking feature was a beautifully carved overmantel about the fireplace, stretching in gleaming oak from floor to ceiling. Cherubs, fruit, musical instruments, an extraordinary array of ornate objects had been worked in the wood, as if the craftsman had wanted to display every facet of his talent in the work. But it had another, quite different quality, in which the carver had shown a more subtle skill. Honoria placed the candle on the hearth and with trembling but sensitive fingers felt her way along the underside of a bunch of grapes, until a slight movement and a faint click showed she had found what she wanted.

'Quickly—over here!' she whispered.

She led the priest to the far corner of the room. Father Swayne had not made the acquaintance of this aspect of their house before. She ran her fingers along the panelling until they had a firm hold, then slid back a whole section, neatly and silently, to reveal a short flight of steps disappearing into the darkness.

'You should be safe there. I'll come and set you free when it's clear.'

He slipped inside, taking his cloak and the bundle of tell-tale objects from the chapel with him. Then Honoria slid the panel shut, secured the concealed fastening in the fireplace, and blew out the candle.

Only just in time. They had turned into the lane now, but the room looked out at the back of the house, and the light would not have been visible to the riders. She ran to her room, and had just dragged off her gown when a thunderous hammering came on the door, and a voice called to open in the King's name.

Feverishly, she pulled off shoes and stockings, unbound her hair, drew back the bed covers and made an impression on the pillow, so that they would think she had been lying there. Then she relit the candle, with dangerously trembling hands, and pulled a loose black velvet gown about her, over her shift.

On the landing she came face to face with Aunt Anne, similarly attired.

'I'll come with you,' her aunt whispered.

'No,' answered Honoria. 'They mustn't think we've any reason to be afraid. Go back to bed, and look surprised and indignant if they search the house.'

Doubtfully, her aunt agreed. But Honoria was glad when Tom came protectively to her side as she reached the hall. It was he who dragged open the door, and let in the man who stood there, and two others bearing torches.

It was not Sir Richard Verney who had ridden through the night to the house, nor any other man she had expected, with his train of pursuivants. However unexpected, it was no stranger who faced her. The torchlight flickered on green and scarlet livery, and threw a grotesque shadow behind the shining head of Sir Gavin Hamilton.

Honoria raised her hand to her mouth with a cry, and stepped back behind Tom's protective form. This was not the man she had last seen half-fainting at his fireside, his eyes softened by her concern for him. His eyes now were hard, bright and unpleasantly amused, and he was in full control of the situation.

'Ah, Mistress Somervell, is it not?' he asked breezily, as if all those previous meetings had never taken place. 'We have reason to believe you are harbouring a priest beneath your roof.'

Honoria drew herself up to her full height, her eyes as bright and hostile as his own. In the torchlight he fancied almost that they flashed green fire. He had imagined many things on his way here, and thought he knew how she would look as he forced his way into her house, but he had not somehow expected this disturbing

combination of pride and courage and defencelessness.
Standing there, slender and still in her pale shift and
sombre gown, her lovely hair loose and heavy about her,
its wonderful colour vibrant and shining in the dim light,
and those beautiful, angry eyes sparkling with hate and
defiance—she had never looked so overwhelmingly
enchanting, nor so completely undefeated.

'You have disturbed our slumbers, sir,' she said, with
an icy calmness she was very far from feeling. 'I must ask
you to leave at once.'

For a moment her assurance almost overturned his
own confidence in his action. Was he wrong? Was there
after all no priest concealed under this roof? Had he
come on a fool's errand?

He pulled himself together almost at once. The
message had been clear and unmistakable: the man had
been quite sure that the Jesuit Father Swayne had
entered the house an hour ago. He summoned his men
indoors with a gesture and ordered them to search every
corner of the manor house and grounds.

Once again Honoria and her aunt and the servants
found themselves herded into the parlour while the
searchers turned the place upside down. Once again
Aunt Anne sat praying while the clamour reached them
from all sides. Once again Honoria endured the anxious
time of waiting, wondering what they would find. This
time there was no Philip to strengthen her courage, and
this time her thoughts were with the man crouched
silently in the dark space behind the panelling, hearing
the sounds, fearful lest they found him there. She had no
illusions: if they found him, he would not suffer alone.
They would all suffer, herself and her aunt, even the
servants. Worse still, any hope Philip might have had
would be finally extinguished, for good and all.

Unless—was this Sir Gavin's latest attempt to force
her into submission, to persuade her that her only escape
was to do as he wanted?

She raised her chin and squared her shoulders and knew that nothing on earth would make her give in. Let him do his worst!

The door was flung open at last, and two of Sir Gavin's men forced their way in, watched anxiously by the occupants of the room. Had they found Father Swayne?

Then Honoria found her arms grasped, and the men dragged her towards the hall.

'Sir Gavin wants you,' one of them said roughly. Her heart beat fast with terror, but she tried not to let it show, even when they closed the door and shut her off from her friends, and left her alone in the hall with her enemy.

She could see at once that he was in a towering rage. His blue eyes blazed with anger as he grasped her shoulders and shook her until the room swayed about her.

'Where is he?' he shouted. 'Where have you hidden him? Damn you, woman, tell me at once—!'

She closed her eyes for a moment to steady herself, then raised them to his face.

'Where is who?' she asked quietly. 'We are all in the parlour.'

His hand swept across and struck her sharply on the cheek.

'Liar! I want the truth—now!'

She raised her hand to rub the red stinging mark, but showed no other sign of fear.

'You know the truth,' she said. 'You will find no one, if you search for ever. Now will you go and leave us? We have enough to do to keep us busy all night, thanks to you.'

He followed her glance to the disorder in the hall, thought of the chaos they had left in every room—even the parlour, for they had searched there, too. He was aware suddenly of the contrast with his own magnificent London house. Here was only sparse, worn furniture, the unmistakable signs of poverty, the evident hardship, which he and his men had done all in their power to increase. He looked at her, knowing that her coolness concealed a great fear. But there was no comfort in that. She and her aunt, an old woman, and three servants, had defied him and his armed retainers. They risked their own safety and freedom, their lives even, to protect the life of another. It was not anger he felt now, but a new and unwanted emotion: somewhere inside him, along with a grudging admiration, flickered the first little impulse of shame he had ever known.

But he suppressed it quickly, and with complete success; and turned his attention again to the woman who faced him.

There was nothing in her eyes now of the gentleness and warmth he had seen at Silston the other day. He knew that she was further away than she had ever been from giving him what he wanted. Her expression was unremittingly hostile. He sensed that if he were to take her in his arms now, she would not melt against him as she had always done before. His action tonight had strengthened all her powers of resistance.

He watched her helplessly, moved as never before by the flawless lines of her face, the entrancing curves of her body, the rich fiery weight of her hair. He must have her! Somehow he must find a way!

But he knew it must be a different way. So far he had made almost no impression on her will. He could no longer hope to reach her through Philip's danger, or her own. Her courage was more than a match for him. He would take a lesson instead from that accident at Silston, and from her words in the barn: 'If I'd given you what you wanted . . . who's to say you'd have raised a finger to help him?' He would show her what he could do, if he chose to use his power in a different manner. And then see if that would move her to let him have his way.

For now, however, he must admit defeat, with as

much dignity as he could muster. He called his men to abandon the search, then bowed with all the nonchalant grace at his command.

'Good night, Mistress Somervell—until we meet again.'

CHAPTER TEN

IN the carved and tapestried library at Belfield Hall, behind richly curtained windows and before a blazing fire almost too warm for the size of the room, Sir Gavin Hamilton completed the formalities of his betrothal to Lady Philomena Sidney. The sweet scent of evergreen boughs filled the air, for Lady Philomena was not so strict a Puritan as to refuse some concession to the Christmas season, and on the wide polished table, beside the legal documents to which the lawyer was putting the final touches, stood dishes of fruit and nuts, a flagon of wine and a silver tray of almond biscuits.

Lady Philomena's richly patterned gown of figured ruby velvet shone glossy in the brilliance of a score of candles, and the same light caught peacock gleams from Sir Gavin's doublet, and emphasised the shining whiteness of the silk shirt revealed through the gold-laced slashes of his sleeves. The floor was partially covered with an oriental carpet, a new fashion, replacing rushes or bare boards with extravagant luxury. The books which gave the room its name were ranged on shelves so elaborately carved that one scarcely noticed what they contained. And outshining all else, on a small table at Lady Philomena's side, stood a vast ornate construction of gold and sapphires over which cherubs climbed and nymphs lay at rest and vine fronds twined their sinuous way. It was Sir Gavin's betrothal gift to his bride. Secretly he thought it extraordinarily vulgar, but his unerring instinct for such things had told him that it was exactly what she would like. Her delighted acceptance of it just now had amply borne out his confidence.

The lawyer's face reflected, with more restraint, the complacent satisfaction of Lady Philomena's expression. She had made a good bargain today, she was sure of that. Her high birth and great fortune had bought her power and influence and, best of all, a young and handsome and charming man who would never have been attracted to her by any other means. An unappealing widow of forty could not have hoped to ensnare him without her undeniable material advantages. From her deeply cushioned chair by the fire she looked up to where he stood, one broad brown hand resting upon the mantelpiece. He was gazing into the fire, his splendid body gracefully at ease: a magnificent figure of a man, a husband to be proud of. Not like her late husband, puny and slow-witted as well as unfaithful. This time it would be different: and she would do all in her power, too, to keep this man for herself. He was hers alone, held by ties firmer than love or sentiment—like him she acknowledged the supremacy of power and gold over other softer values. As her husband he would belong to her, and to no one else, for she wanted no other woman to have any hold over him. She was quite unaware that no woman, least of all herself, had ever had any hold over him at all, since the day when his mother had driven him from her house all those years ago.

So he was reflecting now, as he watched the flames leap about the great logs in the hearth. He would do his duty by Lady Philomena, enough to prevent scandal, but in no other respect would he allow marriage to curtail his freedom. Once again, he thought contentedly, he had used his skill, and his charm and his ruthless will-power to take what he wanted. Just now, putting his signature to his part of the cold-blooded bargain he had felt only triumph and satisfaction that at last it was done, sealed and irrevocable. All that remained was the ostentatious formality of the marriage ceremony. It was a balm to his pride, so recently wounded by Honoria's defiance, to have the sweet taste of victorious ambition in his mouth again.

And yet, now that it was done, he felt slightly sick, cloyed with success, as if he had eaten too many sweetmeats. The complacent glitter in his bride's hard eyes, the over-warm room, the oppressive luxury around him—even the rosy future in which his own comfort and prosperity were assured—somehow these things for which he had worked so hard seemed unpleasantly overpowering. Was it possible to fight tooth and nail for what you wanted, and then find that you did not want it after all? It had never happened to him before, and he did not see why it should have done so now. He could see no flaw in his present happy state.

He moved restlessly to the bookshelves and ran his eyes over the titles marked in gold on the fine leather bindings. Volume after volume of sober and improving reading: sermons, histories with all the spice left out, medical works in the scholar's Latin of which he knew little—any education he had received had come very late, and was hard won, like everything else he had achieved.

He wandered on, running dissatisfied eyes over gloomy portraits and stately tapestries, fingering ornaments and drumming his fingers on every available surface, until he came to his bride's set of virginals, rarely touched, for she was not fond of music. Now he opened them, and sat down and began to play. The words of the song he played tripped lightly through his head:

Shall I come, sweet love, to thee . . ?

An exquisite face took shape in his mind, framed in fiery hair beneath the snowy hood, rosy lips parted in wonder, eyes looking with wide delight on the new worlds opening before them—

He swore under his breath, slammed shut the instrument, and rose to his feet, stumbling over the stool as he did so. Lady Philomena looked round, her self-satisfied mood a little ruffled.

'You are ill at ease, sir,' she said. 'You are eager to be hunting again, I suppose. We will ride together tomorrow, if the weather is kind.'

He came to her side, all smiling affability, and raised her hand to his lips.

'That will be delightful,' he said insincerely. 'We have never yet hunted together.'

'I have heard much of your skill in the hunting field,' she went on, watching him as he moved to a chair facing her, and sat, all courteous attention. Her tone sharpened suddenly: 'But I hope you pursue your quarry more keenly there than you did at Lower Kilworth the other day.'

He gasped, and hoped he had not coloured as deeply as he feared. Her eyes were uncomfortably penetrating.

'Lower Kilworth?' he echoed, trying to look as if he had no idea what she meant. 'Is not that the estate beyond Silston? I don't believe I have hunted there.'

Lady Philomena tapped her foot impatiently.

'Don't play the innocent with me, sir,' she said sharply. 'You know full well what I mean. Your quarry that night was the Jesuit, Father Swayne.'

He smiled warily. What else did she know?

'They have always told me there are no secrets in the country,' he returned with a playful note in his voice. 'But I thought that one was safe. My men are discreet, and Papists are not usually ready to gossip of their hidden dealings. How did you know?'

'As you say, there are no secrets in the country.' She dismissed his question with a gesture, and went on: 'But no wonder you did not want it known. You had nothing to boast of. Why did you leave the place so tamely? If the man's there, he must leave sometime—or they must take him food, or bring messages—something which will give him away. You can get them in the end, one way or another, if you really want to.'

That, he admitted to himself in silence, was the crucial point. He certainly had no interest in the priest's capture. Like Philip Blount, he was a useful tool. Or had seemed so at the time. But it was not an answer likely to impress Lady Philomena. Carefully, he said:

'Ah, but I had another conflicting interest closer to my heart, my lady. Nothing but the greatest danger to the State could have kept me from your side a moment longer, and I do not believe this priest was quite so dangerous as that.'

'That's a matter of opinion,' she said stiffly, but he could see that he had mollified her a little. She might not believe a word of his flattery, but she enjoyed it all the same.

At Lower Kilworth the green boughs of Christmas time only served to emphasise the general shabbiness of the house and the dejection of its inhabitants. Since Sir Gavin's visit there were new scratches, too, new tears in cushions and hangings, new lines scored on plasterwork and panelling. But at least Father Swayne was safe. He had stayed concealed for a few days, eating the food they brought to him after dark, emerging only briefly to breathe the clearer air of the guest bedroom. And then when they were as sure as they could be that the house was no longer watched he left his hiding place and ate a last meal with them before going on his way.

Honoria had hoped once that he might have some advice to give, some new suggestion as to how they might help Philip. But all he could offer were words of strength and comfort. It had to be enough, for Honoria knew there was nothing else. She had not really expected that there would be.

Christmas Day passed quietly, with none of the usual excitement, though they ate more lavishly than at other times, and displayed the expected hospitality to the mummers, doing the rounds of the neighbouring houses. But the thought of Philip cast a shadow over all they did. Neither Honoria nor her aunt slept well these days, and they had little heart for enjoyment. Honoria was troubled, too, to realise how easily tired Anne Blount was, and how small her appetite. She looked far from well. If only they had news, or a letter, it might make the waiting easier to bear.

On Boxing Day morning, as Honoria was discussing the day's meals with Cook, Tom brought her word that a man waited in the stable yard to speak with her. 'News from Philip!' was her first thought, though she did not know whether hope or fear was uppermost in her at the prospect.

But both emotions died away as the man handed her a soft package, too large for a letter and the wrong shape. A new emotion very quickly took their place, however, when he spoke.

'Sir Gavin Hamilton sent this, mistress,' he explained in a low tone.

She looked at him sharply. He was dressed soberly, unobtrusively almost, not in Sir Gavin's flamboyant livery. In fact there was something almost furtive about him, so insignificant was his manner and appearance. One would not look twice at him in passing.

And then Honoria did just that. Was this perhaps the man who had lurked in the trees, to carry word of Father Swayne's arrival? The possibility almost drove the thought of what he brought out of her head.

But only for a moment. She looked down at what she held, carefully wrapped in white silk and bound with a green ribbon. It was unmistakably a gift. Or was it something else, and he wanted her to believe it was a gift?

As if she thought it might contain a snake she thrust it back quickly into the man's hands.

'I want nothing from him,' she said. 'I cannot imagine why he should think I would.'

Undeterred, the man held out the package again.

'He said, mistress,' he explained in that same confiding tone, 'that it was by way of a peace-offering, if you would take it in that spirit.'

She was silent for a moment, and then asked guardedly:

'Do you know what he meant by that?'

'No, mistress. But he said I was to leave it with you and not wait.'

Slowly she took the package and held it, feeling along its length, but she could not guess what it contained. She was reluctant to open it before this man, in case Sir Gavin had planned to humiliate her in some way, but she was equally unwilling to let him go, in case she wanted to return the gift to its sender. In the end she was spared the decision, for the man bowed and took his leave and before she could say another word had left her standing alone in the stable yard with the package in her hands.

Avoiding curious glances she ran quickly to her room and closed the door and set to work with trembling hands to undo the ribbon—very carefully, for her economical mind recognised that it might come in useful in their impoverished household. She folded it and laid it aside and then, slowly, cautiously, she unwrapped the silk to see what lay inside. Something soft, and shining, and delicately perfumed—

An exclamation of delight escaped her, and she lifted out the gloves which lay there. She had never in all her life, she thought, seen a pair so beautiful: of finest white kid lined with silk, and finished in white satin, silken fringed and embroidered with an exquisitely intricate pattern of leaves and stems in a pretty green, bright and fresh as new beech leaves. Somehow the design made her think of meadow grass on a frosty morning, when every blade is edged with silver filigree. She could not imagine anything more to her taste than these. She slipped them on, delighting in the perfect fit, the soft suppleness on her hands, the subtle fragrance with which they were impregnated.

And then she remembered who had sent them. Their charm vanished in an instant. She pulled them off, and laid them on the bed and regarded them with disfavour. Why on earth had he suddenly taken it into his head to send her this expensive and tasteful gift?

She gazed down at her hands, noting how red and worn they were: quite unfitted for such beautiful gloves. But, she thought ruefully, at least they would be well-hidden beneath that soft leather. Perhaps that was it. She remembered his eyes running over her that day in the barn, taking in critically every aspect of her appearance: and in her enjoyment of the unexpected sunshine that morning she had ridden out without gloves. Possibly he thought she possessed none. She blushed uncomfortably at the reflection.

'He said it was by way of a peace-offering, if you would take it in that spirit.' The words came suddenly to mind, scarcely heard when the man spoke them, so astonished had she been. A 'peace-offering': for what? For that nocturnal visit, and the chaos he had left behind? For all the distress of mind he had caused her since their first meeting? Or was it not really intended as a peace-offering at all, but simply as a new way to woo her, to lure her more firmly than ever into his snare? Many women were easily tempted by such things.

But not Honoria. Tight-lipped, she wrapped them again in the silk, and tied the ribbon about them, and laid them in the furthest corner of the carved oak press in her room. And tried very hard to forget that they were there.

Only Tom had seen the man come that day, and all he

said to her, in an undertone, as she crossed the yard some hours later, was: 'I could swear that was the fellow I saw in the lane.'

There was sickness in the hamlet of Lower Kilworth, two miles from the Manor. One after another the members of each household went down with a low fever, which left them weak and listless on the slow road to recovery. But it was a mild fever: the only deaths were among the already sickly, the very young and the very old. It kept Honoria occupied, though, trudging her way from cottage to cottage with eggs and broth and home-made remedies, her gentle voice and quiet soothing manner as welcome as the gifts she brought. It was a relief to her, as well as to those she visited, to have something useful to do. A relief to be too busy to think of all the bewildering and dreadful things which had happened since that night in November. Scarcely two months had passed since then, yet it seemed like a lifetime.

The short winter day was almost at an end as she made her way home one afternoon a week after the outbreak began, her empty basket over her arm and her tired feet carrying her more slowly than she might have chosen. The wind was sharp with frost, and found its way only too easily through the folds of her cloak. She looked forward to the warm fire at the other end of the lane, and thought a little anxiously of Aunt Anne: she had been slightly feverish herself this morning.

The low sun, round and red on the horizon, shone straight into her eyes as she turned into the Manor Lane, barred by the stark black lines of the winter trees which edged the road. She wondered bleakly if Philip would ever again see the evening sun fall in a blazing ball beyond the rim of the world, or walk at her side up the lane to their home. Would she ever see him again in this life?

She was so deep in her sad reflections that she did not

hear the approaching rider until he was almost upon her. Then she turned swiftly, startled by the thud of hooves on the muddy ground just behind her.

The rosy gold of the setting sun shone full on him, magnifying his splendour so that she almost exclaimed in wonder at it. Like a hero of ancient times he bore down upon her on his proud grey stallion. Copper-coloured now in the magical light, his splendid golden head was set with arrogance upon his broad shoulders, his tawny velvet cloak thrown back as if he did not feel the cold like lesser mortals. She held her breath and gazed at him with eyes full of awe.

Then she gave a little shake, and reminded herself that he was only a man, and one she had every reason to hate. She stood aside to let him pass.

'There are still no priests at Lower Kilworth,' she pointed out with asperity. 'But perhaps you do not need an excuse to persecute defenceless women.'

In the sunset light she could not see if his colour deepened or not, but she had an impression that he looked a little shamefaced for a moment. Then he smiled, drew rein and dismounted. At her side he was human again at once, Sir Gavin Hamilton muddying his fine boots in the Manor Lane. But unfortunately no less disquieting for that. Why did she always suffer that unpleasant breathlessness in his company?

'Ah, I come on quite another errand this time, Mistress Somervell. But I did not expect to find you out of doors so late.'

She explained where she had been, trying not to meet his gaze—it was so hard to look at him without blushing. He made no comment when she had finished speaking, but she felt his eyes travel over her, and was aware, uncomfortably, that they had come to rest on her hands, clad in the plain worn sheepskin gloves she had owned for years.

'You do not wear them, I see,' he observed, in a

non-committal tone. She glanced up at him. She was not sure, but she fancied he looked slightly hurt. Though that was hard to believe. Just in case, she said gently:

'They are much too good for such common wear as this.'

She was quite sure this time that he looked relieved.

'You accept my peace-offering then?'

She turned to face him and stood still.

'Peace-offering for what?' she asked.

There was a little silence. She sensed somehow that it had nothing to do with what they were saying. She looked up at him, aware with a new intensity of the strong column of his neck rising firm and brown from the stiff white collar, of the strength of his jaw, the high curve of his cheekbone limned by the rosy light, the smudged lines of his straight brows, and the softening outline of long dark lashes about the blue eyes, the supple warmth of his mouth beneath the arrogant nose. She saw the chill night wind ruffle the thickness of his hair where it curled on the nape of his neck, and found herself longing all at once to touch him there, to slide her fingers into the springing gold, to feel his arm draw her nearer, his lips on hers.

She shivered, and pulled her cloak about her more securely, as if she could shut out unwanted impulses as easily as she could keep out the wind: which was not very effectively in either case. He moved then, and smiled, and remembered her question.

'Whatever you choose,' he said. 'I intended it as a symbol, shall we say.' Seeing her about to speak again, he enlarged: 'Let the past take care of itself. We make a new start, you and I.'

She wondered if his words were meant as some kind of oblique apology, but she was not sure. He was not the apologising kind. She smiled grimly at the very thought, but she was no nearer understanding him.

'What are you trying to say?' she demanded, a little

impatiently, shivering again, but only with cold this time.

He spread his hands expressively.

'Never mind,' he said. 'Suffice it to say that I am a new man, as far as you are concerned.'

'Oh?' she commented warily. She was not sure that she liked the sound of that. Not, she reminded herself, that the old one was altogether to her taste.

He began to walk on slowly, leading his horse, and she went with him. He seemed to be seeking the right words, for after a pause he said:

'I am going to Court in a week or two.'

'Oh?' There did not seem to be any appropriate comment.

'If you were to make an appearance I could ensure that you had the King's ear. If you still wish it.'

She stood absolutely still and gazed at him.

'Wish it?' she echoed breathlessly. 'You mean . . . for Philip . . . ?' She dared not speak aloud, for fear she had misunderstood him.

He nodded, and cleared his throat.

'Yes,' he said. 'I cannot promise complete success—'

'Once you did,' she broke in sharply.

'As I say,' he went on, ignoring the interruption, 'I cannot promise that you will save Master Blount. But it is possible—likely—I would add the weight of my word to yours—'

She clasped her hands together, her eyes bright with hope.

'Oh . . . oh! I don't know what to say! Do you mean it, really and truly? Would you—?' Tears leapt to the surface, and roughened her voice. 'Oh, sir, if only you would!'

He bowed, with a flourish of his broad-brimmed hat.

'I shall be glad to be of service, mistress,' he returned. He smiled slightly, but enigmatically, meeting her excitement with distant courtesy. 'Further,' he went on, 'should you need a new gown for your appearance at Court—'

'I am not too proud to wear my old clothes,' she interposed with a faint note of hauteur. He remembered how she had looked at their first meeting, and acknowledged silently that she had no need of his help in this. He bowed again.

'As you please, mistress.' Then he said: 'It is growing late. Let us go in to your aunt.'

As they reached the house the last lingering glow of the sunset hovered on the horizon, and then was gone.

CHAPTER
ELEVEN

THE next days passed in a ferment of excitement and uncertainty for Honoria. Sir Gavin had given her no explanation for his change of heart, and made no conditions. But for all the sudden upsurge of hope she could not trust him: not after all that had happened. She had promised him nothing, but she was deeply suspicious that this was some new ruse of his to lure her to his bed.

Yet his manner in the lane that day had been very different from his bearing towards her in the past: without harshness or threats or passion. He had been cool and courteous, subdued almost. She felt, obscurely, almost disappointed that his behaviour had been so correct—which was surely foolish and quite beyond her understanding. After all, what he offered her seemed, on the surface, to be exactly what she wanted. Though not until she saw the King and spoke to him face to face would she believe that Sir Gavin had meant what he said.

For that reason she tried not to raise Anne Blount's hopes too much. She could not, of course, prevent her from knowing that she was to go to London to make one last attempt to save Philip's life, and from sending her on her way with the most fervent prayers for her success. But Honoria impressed upon her that success was by no means certain. It was a chance, no more. She was glad at least that her aunt seemed a little better, for she would not have liked to leave her otherwise.

So towards the end of January she and Tom set out again on the road to London. This time, with Sir Gavin's help, she carried all the necessary papers, giving her permission, Catholic though she was, to travel so far from home. He had sent them to her before leaving for London himself. She had not seen him since that night in the lane. This time, too, Uncle William Somervell had been warned of her coming and was ready to welcome her to his comfortable house.

She had been there two days when a letter from Sir Gavin informed her that his coach would be at the door the next morning to take her to Whitehall. It was the first time she had seen his writing, but somehow the bold and yet careful script was exactly what she would have expected. She studied it for some time, reading many shades of tone and meaning into the two brief sentences it contained. What had he felt as he wrote it? Simple pleasure at being able to help her? She dismissed that possibility at once. With Sir Gavin nothing was ever simple, except his overriding self-interest. And yet if her meeting with the King brought about Philip's release, what did it matter if Sir Gavin's motives were of the darkest? She could only be deeply and eternally grateful to him. She had not led him to expect anything more than that.

The next day dawned cold and cheerless, one of those bitter winter days when it scarcely seemed to grow light at all. But at Whitehall, when the coach left Honoria and her uncle there, the numberless crowded rooms were brilliant with candles, noisy and warm and bustling. How, thought Honoria, would they ever find Sir Gavin—or the King, come to that—in all this throng? Or even, for that matter, find their way out again. Courtiers, petitioners, townsfolk and countrymen, bare-breasted maidens and haughty matrons, crying children and old men sleeping in corners: she thought half the nation must be here today. But there was no sign of Sir Gavin.

Her uncle, more worldly-wise than she, elbowed a

path through the crowds and led her to a wider, more elaborately furnished room which was clearly some kind of ante-chamber, though it was, if anything, more thick with people than the rooms through which they had passed. Honoria felt that by the time she reached the King the black velvet of her gown would be crushed beyond recovery, and her hair falling loose in untidy clusters about her hot face.

Then a hand grasped her arm. She turned quickly to look into the neatly bearded face of a sprucely dressed man she did not know. Before she could reveal her disappointment, he said:

'Mistress Somervell? If you will be so good as to come this way His Majesty will see you now.'

Her uncle was told, politely, that he need not wait. Mistress Somervell would be given an appropriate escort to see her home when she was ready. Honoria watched him go with mixed feelings. She felt suddenly very alone.

Her guide led her through two more rooms to a third, where the painted ceiling and long windows indicated that she had reached her destination at last. Here the crowds were not so pressing, for all that they were as great. Courtiers stood about in little groups, orderly and less noisy than in the ante-chambers. Close by, three children stood with attendant servants. She guessed who they were by their rich clothes, even before her companion whispered in her ear:

'His Royal Highness, Henry, Prince of Wales,' he indicated the fair, good-looking boy of about eleven, strongly made and completely at ease. 'A most hopeful prince,' enlarged the man approvingly. Then: 'Her Royal Highness the Princess Elizabeth.' She was a lively dark-eyed nine year old, already promising a startling beauty. 'And the little Prince Charles,' the man's voice held a faintly pitying note now, appropriate to the slight sickly-looking five year old, who could scarcely walk even yet, so she was told, and who spoke with a painful stammer. Wide, sad dark eyes seemed to gaze from his small pale face into a gloomy future, far removed from that on which his brother and sister looked, laughing together at his side. Honoria watched the three of them with interest for a moment or two, and then began to look about the room again.

And there, thank God, was Sir Gavin, coming her way: he had not misled her after all. She caught her breath at his splendour. He was wearing a doublet of peacock satin which would have looked overpowering on any lesser man, such as, for example, the man who leaned confidingly on his arm at this moment, a plumpish brown-haired scant-bearded man in silver-grey, with a black cloak, crimson lined, and a large diamond in his otherwise undistinguished hat. He was not much shorter than Sir Gavin, but Honoria thought with almost proprietory pride that her enemy—or was he now her friend?—overshadowed him completely.

They had seen her, and were making their way through the other courtiers towards her. As they came men and women drew aside, and bowed, and flourished their hats.

It was then that Honoria realised with a little shock that it was not Sir Gavin, for all his regal splendour, who drew these attentions from the crowd, but that ordinary-looking man at his side, for it was he who turned from side to side to acknowledge the courtesies. She was face to face at last with the son of the beautiful and tragic Mary Queen of Scots, for whom so many of her faith had given their lives: James, the Sixth of that name in Scotland, now by the grace of God King of England. The man in whose hands Philip's future lay, and her happiness. Just in time she came to her senses and sank to the floor in a deep curtsey.

They came to a halt just before her, and she looked up to meet the penetrating gaze of a pair of shrewd light blue eyes. Unimpressive though he was, the King was quite clearly no fool. Now his small mouth curved in a smile of amused approval, and he gave a sideways glance at his companion.

'So this is my Gavin's wee lassie,' he said. His accent was far more broadly Scots than Sir Gavin's. But then his favourite had worked hard to soften his tones, in a Court which regarded his countrymen with suspicion.

Honoria blushed to hear herself termed a 'wee lassie'—and in no sense, either, she thought angrily, do I belong to Sir Gavin. But she schooled herself to accept the description without changing her expression.

She was astonished when the King relinquished Sir Gavin's support, and came forward to take her hand and raise her to her feet.

'Let's take a look at you now,' he said, and proceeded to do just that, with what she hoped was approbation. Then he took her chin in his hand and turned her face this way and that, as if to study it carefully from all angles. 'A bonny lass,' he observed at last, releasing her. 'A pity indeed she should be a Papist, eh Gavin?'

'Ah, but I think she would claim, nevertheless, sire,' put in Sir Gavin, 'that she is in all other things your most loyal and devoted subject.'

The King turned back to Honoria.

'You hear that, maid? You have a friend at my side. But I ask why, if indeed you are loyal to your King, you do not serve him also in religion, as in all else?'

Honoria thought quickly, then replied:

'Is it not written, sire: "Render unto Caesar the things that are Caesar's and unto God the things that are God's"?'

The King laughed delightedly, and slapped his thigh.

'Well said, lassie, well said! A girl after my own heart, Gavin—' And then the smile disappeared as quickly as it had come, and he leant towards her. 'But if you are told that your God demands disloyalty to your King, what then?'

'I would not believe it, sire,' she said, her eyes meeting his, level and unafraid. 'And neither would my cousin, Master Philip Blount.' She held her breath then, waiting for his response, hoping that she had not been presumptuous in bringing before him so soon what was uppermost in her mind.

She was relieved when the King smiled, albeit a trifle wryly.

'Ah, the gentleman in the Tower: I thought we should come to that. But dare you speak of him to me, maid? No man who has plotted treason can hope for mercy.'

'Nor would I ask it, sire, if that were so,' she said, and fell again in a soft graceful movement to her knees. Her voice was warm and vibrant with emotion, and tears trembled on her long lashes. 'Sire,' she said, 'I can speak for him as I can for myself. I swear by all I hold most dear that he is, and always has been, your loyal and loving subject. His only crime was that of friendship with a man who was not so loyal. But never was my cousin a party to that horrible conspiracy, nor knew of it. I beg that you, sire, in your great mercy will be moved to set him free, and I promise that he and I will serve you faithfully and with love to the end of our days.'

A hush fell over the room as she spoke, for her passionate tones carried beyond the little group about the King and many heads were turned to see who was pleading so eloquently.

The King raised her once more to her feet, his expression thoughtful.

'You plead his case well,' he said. 'You are to wed him, is that not so?' She nodded silently, for the flood of words had used up all her resources. She felt close to weeping now. 'As bonny a lass as you are should be wed, and that soon,' he commented. Her heart gave a little leap of joy and hope. Did that mean she had won? But he said only: 'We shall give the matter our full consideration. Be sure that if his case warrants it, then he will receive our mercy. If not—then I hope that you will nevertheless remain our loyal subject, learning from your cousin's fate that it is not prudent to conspire against your King.'

She did not know how to take his words. She only curtsied and said faintly: 'I thank you, sire,' and watched him walk away, his attention already on something else. She thought he and Sir Gavin were talking of hunting as they left her.

She stood where she was, bewildered and suddenly very tired. What was she to do now? All she wanted was to find somewhere quiet where she could be alone, and give way to her tears, and somehow renew her strength to face the waiting hours or days before she could hope to know the King's decision. There was not even a seat here where she could sink down and rest until the trembling in her limbs had subsided a little.

Then a hand touched her arm, and Sir Gavin was beside her. She was almost ready to lay her head on his broad shoulder and weep there, with his strong arm about her. But that was foolish, and clearly very far from his thoughts, though he said approvingly:

'You did well. The King was pleased with you. As for Master Blount, we must wait and see. The trial of the conspirators is to take place on Monday, so whatever happens you will not have too long to wait. That is always the worst part.' She tried to force a smile, to thank him for his practical, comforting tone, but it was a very watery effort, scarcely recognisable as such. He linked her arm through his. 'The coach is waiting,' he said. 'I'll take you there now, and you can go straight home.'

They made their way through the crowded rooms in silence. Honoria reflected that it was a strange and new experience to find his presence so comforting, to feel only safe and protected because he was there. But then his was the sole familiar face in this frightening rabbit-warren of a palace, and he had acted as a friend today, whatever he had been yesterday, and might be tomorrow.

When they reached the open air at last and stood by the waiting coach she turned to look at him and gave him her hand saying warmly:

'Thank you, sir. I can only be grateful for the part you played today.'

He bowed over her hand with the same airy courtesy he had shown in the lane.

'You know I am your devoted servant,' he said lightly. 'As always.' His eyes were bright and full of laughter, and she did not know how to take his words. She had never felt less mistrustful of him than she did at this moment, and yet she could not even now be sure of his intentions.

She turned to step into the coach, then stood still suddenly, her eye caught by a man glimpsed in the crowd. She laid a hand urgently on her companion's arm.

'That man, Sir Gavin—over there, by the lady in green—the man with pale hair and pock marks—do you see him?'

Gavin followed her gaze, and nodded, with a slightly puzzled air.

'Yes. What of him?'

'I thought,' she said, raising her eyes to his, 'that he might be a man of yours, set to watch me. I have seen him often before—and I think he was seen at home one day, in the market.' She shivered. 'Do you know him?'

He shook his head.

'I don't remember ever seeing him in my life before,' he said. 'Perhaps he's one of Salisbury's men. I shouldn't be alarmed, if I were you. Are you not always telling me your conscience is clear?'

'So it is,' she replied, a little tartly. The old irritation stirred within her for a moment, then she thought how ungrateful she was to feel like that, and thanked him again, and allowed him to hand her into the coach and see her on her way.

CHAPTER
TWELVE

On Monday 27th January at Westminster Hall the trial of the Gunpowder conspirators took place.

Honoria knew of it, of course, if only because Sir Gavin had told her of it. But no word had reached her yet of the King's decision, nothing to assure her that Philip was not there with those other men, on trial for his life.

'You are not to go out,' said her uncle, with more than his customary firmness, when in her restlessness she longed for fresh air. 'It's no time for Papists to be on the streets. If anyone recognised you—' He left the sentence unfinished, but Honoria shivered all the same. 'The crowds are in an ugly mood. Don't tempt fate: stay safe within doors until after—' he amended the sentence hurriedly '—for a few days more.'

What he meant, she knew, was 'until after the executions'. The trial was a formality, a mere public display. The men had been tried and condemned almost from the moment of their arrest, certainly during the long weeks of questioning and torture in the Tower. The executions would follow as a matter of course, very soon.

Honoria hoped that her uncle would make enquiries for her, find out if Philip was among those prisoners ranged before the hostile onlookers at Westminster. Perhaps he would have done, fond as he had become of her in the short time they had known each other, but on the day preceding the trial he took to his bed with a severe chill and would not allow her near him for fear of infection. Jane Porter ministered to his needs, and the other servants were too taken up with their increased duties to pay much heed to Honoria. In any case she could not have asked them for news: she sensed that even they shared the present fashionable shrinking from all of her faith. That as much as anything encouraged her to heed her uncle's warning and stay within doors.

Surely, surely, she thought, Sir Gavin will send word. But the days passed with painful slowness and still there was no news. In her uncle's house she did not even hear reports of the trial, the only points of interest discussed before her being William Somervell's progress: 'He had a bad night, poor gentleman,' 'Yes, I think him a little better today,' 'He managed some broth this evening.'

As if, thought Honoria impatiently, his indisposition could be more important than Philip's life, even now perhaps nearing its close. In the general interest in the vagaries of her uncle's appetite no one seemed to notice that she was not eating either, though that at least did not trouble Honoria. It was not for herself that she paced the floor in a fever of anxiety and fear.

Thursday came, and the early morning bustle in the street outside was succeeded by an expectant hush which lasted some hours before the daily noise was resumed. On Friday the tension in the air was more marked, and the sounds of a great crowd passing beneath her window woke Honoria before daybreak.

She looked out and saw a vast eddying mass of people travelling all in the same direction along the street, laughing, chattering, shouting, in a clamorous holiday mood which yet had an edge of quivering excitement, emphasised by the lurid uncertain glare of torches set in sconces here and there to light the street. Later, Honoria recognised that she had known all along what drew them so surely that one way. But for now she thought only that she must go and join them, must ask for news. Out in the street there would doubtless be someone to tell her what she had to know.

She dressed quickly and pulled a cloak about her, then crept down to let herself out of the house before anyone could know she was no longer in bed. The wind was cold, and a grey light was slowly filling the sky. The crowd seemed greater now, and she stood watching them pass, wondering how she could ever manage to slip in amongst them. Then a woman stumbled, and paused to right herself, and Honoria darted into the space that formed briefly in front of her.

It was as if she had been caught up in a raging torrent, for she could no more have turned aside now than she could have tried to swim against the relentless pull of a river in flood. She was jostled and pushed and dragged forward, on and on where the hurrying feet were moving as one, where excitement and eagerness and anticipation were carrying each one of those around her. The noise was overwhelming, so great that she felt she could not have made her voice heard above it if she had wanted to ask where they were going and why. But what she heard when a passing remark caught her ears was enough to keep her silent. And enough, too, for her to regret bitterly that she had not taken her uncle's advice and stayed at home.

'Down with all bloody Papists, say I,' a man near her said to his wife, who nodded bright-eyed agreement. 'I'd hang the lot of them if I had my way,' that from another. 'They're all the same, they'd have us all burnt at the stake'—'Aye, and force us all into nasty superstitious foreign ways.' A third man spat in disgust, just missing her foot: 'Any trouble, and you can be sure it's the Papists behind it,' he said. Their hatred seemed to envelope her, holding her as surely as their moving bodies, drowning, stifling her.

She tried to turn, struggling wildly, her arms reaching up as if to clutch at the open sky far above the crowding heads with their hate-filled eyes. But hands pushed and clawed at her, voices asked roughly what she thought she

was doing, feet caught at her legs and tripped her. She
had a sudden nightmare fear of falling, crushed under
the hurrying feet of the heedless crowd. She gave in and
turned again to let them carry her where they were
going.

After what seemed long hours of that bewildering
journey their pace slowed at last. Voices were hushed,
heads raised to peer above the crowd. The excitement
grew, but it was a silent emotion now. The narrow street
through which they were passing ended in a wide open
area, edged by houses whose every window was
thronged with people. On all sides below the crowd
stretched, so that it did not seem possible that another
space could be found for one more human being. And
there, far across the yard above the eager watching
heads, stood the scaffold, high and new and waiting,
built so that everyone who was there could have a
perfect view of the drama to be enacted upon it.

There was no hope of turning now, though with every
fibre of her being Honoria longed to be anywhere but
here. She had been inexorably destined to stand in this
dreadful place from the moment when she took that first
fatal step into the passing crowd. Why, oh why had she
done it? What else but this could have brought all these
people hurrying through the streets before dawn, eager
to secure a place? What else would have brought the old
and the young, the fathers with children on their
shoulders, the sober citizens and their wives, the whores
and thieves and beggars, the nobles and gentlemen and
ladies of the court to wait for hours for the spectacle to
begin? Though those last, she noticed, had the places of
honour in the windows overlooking the square: was Sir
Gavin there somewhere, talking to the ladies, wine in his
hand and a dish of sweetmeats at his elbow?

Now she was here she could only stand where the
crowd held her and wait until it was time to leave. And
that would not be until . . . She covered her face with her

hands and shuddered, great waves of horror running over her.

Beside her, a man looked round and nudged her with his arm.

'What's up, wench? Feeling bad?'

She could not tell him the truth. What would they do to her if they knew, in their present ugly mood? She wondered fleetingly if after all they might make a way for her to escape if she said she felt ill, but she could see how dense the crowds were on all sides of her. She was more likely to be crushed underfoot if she tried to move. Instead she uncovered her face and tried to smile, and shook her head. The man lost interest and turned away.

Far off a drum sounded, insistent, coming steadily nearer. A ripple of excitement ran through the crowd and a ragged jeering cry rose in the distance. But from here they could see nothing until at last the doomed cavalcade reached the scaffold.

There was a little group forming on the platform now. 'Thomas Wintour,' said someone near her, 'He's first.' One of the men detached himself from the group and came forward to speak briefly to the crowd, unheard so far away as this, then he paused for a moment in prayer, and slowly, unsteadily, mounted the grim ladder to the noose that swayed in the gusty wind. Honoria's horrified eyes were held against her will as he dropped and swung, jerking, for all too short a time before they cut him down. She had met him once, in Robin Catesby's company. Now the rolling drums could not drown the ghastly cries, and the horrible yelping triumph of the mob, like hounds thirsting for the kill.

The sky seemed to rock, and the house tops and the crowd with it, lurching from side to side as if an earthquake shook them. Faster and faster, blurring into greyness, closing in as she fell. 'I am drowning,' she thought as the darkness swallowed her up and she fell for ever into the bottomless abyss.

'Clear a way there! Get back, man, can't you see the lady's not well?' The voice penetrated the darkness, dispersing it slowly. She was aware of strong arms holding her in a firm grasp above the swaying ground, aware of the softness of velvet beneath her cheek, aware that by some miracle the crowd was parting, letting them through.

Then it dawned on her that it was not the world which had been swaying so sickeningly, but herself. She must have fainted where she stood, overwhelmed by the horrors she was witnessing. Now these strong arms were carrying her to safety and she was free of the vile baying mob. She could hear them still, shouting their words of hate, the sound rising to a ghastly crescendo in unison with the reverberating drums.

'Philip . . .' she murmured faintly, struggling to look round.

'No . . . no,' a deep familiar voice soothed her. 'It's Guy Fawkes now. It's nearly over.'

They must have turned into a side street, for it was suddenly quiet, the noise of the crowd falling to a distant roar. Gently, Sir Gavin set her down on a mounting block against a wall and knelt to rub her cold hands between his strong warm palms. Honoria tried to control the shuddering which threatened to overwhelm her, and gazed at him numbly.

'I knew him too,' she whispered through white lips. She remembered the devout Yorkshireman with eager eyes: what were they doing to him now?

'Hush—don't talk of it,' Gavin urged her. 'You should not be here at all,' he went on. 'It's no place for you today.'

Her mouth was dry, and she could scarcely speak, but there was one question she must ask, the one she had longed to have answered for days now.

'Philip—' she began again. 'Is he—was he—?'

He looked bewildered for a moment, and then

understood her and shook his head, saying quickly:

'Oh no, those were the chief conspirators today—the lesser men were hanged yesterday—but not Philip,' he added, seeing her already pale face turn ashen with horror. He sat back on his heels and held her hands in his. 'But did you not know?'

'No,' she replied. Her voice still came in scarcely more than a whisper. 'My uncle has been ill—'

'I know,' he said. 'I've just come from there.'

She looked up sharply.

'You have? Why, is something wrong?' Her tone was edged with anguish now. 'Oh, sir, have you news?'

He smiled gently.

'Better than that,' he said. She scarcely took in the words, but his tone brought her a little comfort. 'If you think you are fit to move,' he went on, 'Then let us go back.'

He glanced behind him and gave a shout, and she saw that two of his men waited on horseback some distance away beside the grey stallion he had ridden when they met in the lane at Lower Kilworth.

She rose unsteadily to her feet, and his arm was about her waist, supporting her as she crossed the street to where the horse was tethered. And then in a single movement—she never quite knew how—he lifted her into the saddle and held her there while he swung himself up behind her.

For a moment she sat stiffly upright, the old alarm rising sharply in her, but his arm came about her and drew her gently back to rest against him. She was too tired to resist and his hold on her was firm, and safe, the warmth of his strong body greatly comforting. He urged his horse forward at a slow pace and Honoria closed her eyes. Once she thought she felt his mouth against her hair, but it must have been an illusion, for he spoke almost at once, his voice quietly matter-of-fact.

'This wind's bitterly cold: are you warm enough?'

'Yes, thank you,' she replied. Then she went on: 'I thought you would be there, watching, like the other great folk.'

She felt him shrug his shoulders.

'Such things don't interest me,' he said off-handedly, as if, she thought, the dreadful deaths of men she had known were of no significance. But she was too grateful to him just now to be angry.

She thought she must have been carried miles away from her uncle's house today, but in no time at all Sir Gavin was reining in the horse and saying: 'Here we are.' He dismounted and reached up to lift her down after him. Just for a moment he let his hands linger on her waist as if to steady her, but when she looked up, about to speak, he released her and gave her his arm to lead her into the house.

Once in the hall he stood still with an abruptness which startled her, and an odd unaccountable expression on his face.

'Go into the parlour,' he said quietly.

She gazed at him curiously.

'But won't you come and take some refreshment? After your kindness today it seems only right.'

'Soon,' he said. 'You go first.' He gave her a little push. For a moment she hung back, then a new, wild, incredible hope surged through her. She flung a speechless question to him with her eyes, and thought she read the answer in his. Then in the pause between one breath and the next she turned and ran across the hall and pushed open the parlour door.

He was there. Seated patiently at the fireside, grey-faced and thin and ill, but with a look of immense contentment on his weary face. Philip, her beloved, whom she had thought never to see again in life.

He looked round and colour warmed his face, and then he rose awkwardly to his feet and stood facing her, steadying himself on the back of the chair.

She gave a great cry and ran to clasp him in her arms, sobbing and laughing together, joyful incoherent words pouring from her in a torrent, and his arms closed about her with gentle thankfulness.

Then she remembered how unwell he looked, and drew back, and saw that he was scarcely able to stand, that only will-power kept him still upright.

'Sit down, my dear,' she urged him tenderly, and when he did so knelt on the floor beside him and laid her head in his lap. They sat like that in silence for a long time, while his hand stroked her hair and she allowed the wonderful and overwhelming happiness of their reunion to flow through her in a warm tide.

They were still like that when Sir Gavin came in, cautiously, but encouraged by Philip's welcoming smile. It was not until her cousin spoke that Honoria even realised that Gavin was there.

'We have so much to thank you for, sir,' said Philip's quiet voice. 'More than we can ever hope to repay.'

She raised her head and looked round, and caught Sir Gavin's eyes on her. He looked more sombre than she had ever seen him before, frowning a little, his eyes holding no trace of their accustomed lightness. She smiled, anxious to coax him into sharing their joy, for after all he had brought it to them, then she rose to her feet.

'Sit down, sir, and we'll drink together.' She turned to the table where cakes and wine had been set ready, and filled three glasses. Behind her she heard Sir Gavin explaining, rather stiffly, how and where he had found her. She gathered that he had brought Philip in his own coach when he was released from the Tower this morning, and had been dismayed to learn that Honoria had disappeared from her uncle's house. If one of the servants had not glimpsed her from the window as the crowd caught her up he might never have found her.

She brought wine to the two of them, saying with a shudder:

'It was horrible, Philip.' Her cousin's eyes told her that he understood what she must have suffered.

'There were men no more guilty than I who died yesterday,' he said quietly.

'Then be thankful you were not among them,' returned Sir Gavin. Honoria cast a swift glance in his direction: she thought he sounded almost annoyed.

'We are both thankful,' she told him. 'And we know whom we have to thank.'

He stood up, his glass in his hand, and went to the window, turning his back on them both.

'The King,' he said brusquely, 'and your own eloquence.'

She gazed at him in bewilderment. What had happened to make him so surly, at this moment when he had brought her so much joy? It took a little of the edge from her happiness to think that he was offended in some way. Yet he had no reason that she knew of to be offended.

'No,' she protested, 'we owe it all to you. If it had not been for your help—Philip, I don't suppose you know all he has done—'

'I found out a little on the way here. But it required very close questioning.' He smiled. 'You are modest, sir, but I know well enough that I owe you my life.'

Sir Gavin did turn round then, and even smiled with cool politeness, bowing his head to acknowledge Philip's gratitude. But all he said was:

'I must take my leave of you now. Remember what I advised, Master Blount, and return home as soon as you can: you have all the necessary papers. London is no place for your kind at the moment.'

His tone was brisk and practical and completely lacking in warmth.

'Must you go?' pleaded Honoria. 'We owe you more

thanks than this.'

'Not at all,' he demurred. He bowed to her and turned away.

'I'll come with you to the door,' she said.

She ignored his protest and went with him, but he walked so quickly that she did not catch up with him until he had reached the front door. He paused then and looked at her, and she felt chilled by the indifference in his eyes.

'There was really no need,' he said. 'I know my way.'

She laid her hand on his arm.

'I wish we could make you understand how deeply grateful we are,' she said warmly. 'You have shown yourself more than generous.'

He shook off her hand and reached out to open the door.

'Goodbye, Mistress Somervell. Don't linger in London. You will be safer at home. If you use the services of a priest for your marriage to Master Blount take due care.'

She smiled at that, but there was no answering amusement in his eyes. She thought he would go then with no further word, but all at once he relinquished the latch and turned to face her. There was a strange light in his eyes and she shrank back a little, suddenly afraid.

'I must—' he began, and then broke off and without warning seized her in his arms.

He held her fiercely, so that she could scarcely breathe, and she struggled feebly for a moment. 'One last kiss,' he said urgently, and then his mouth came down on hers, hard and fierce and demanding.

She ceased to struggle now, for she no longer wanted to. Her arms reached out and closed about him, and she gave herself up to his embrace. She felt every bone of her body melt against him as if they two had become fused into one, felt his hands caress her, waking her to blazing life beneath his touch, felt his mouth force her lips apart in eager response to his passionate insistence.

He had never kissed her like this before. Even that first time, when she had learned from him the meaning of passion, even then he had not come to her with this desperate demanding hunger. His whole being seemed to scorch her with a ruthless flame of desire, devouring, devastating, setting her instantly, wildly, fiercely alight.

When at last he drew away from her she was trembling uncontrollably, left suddenly desolate. She longed for him to take her in his arms again, but he only cupped her face in gentle hands, and said softly:

'Goodbye, Mistress Somervell.'

And then he brushed her lips lightly with his own and was gone.

She stood for a long time gazing at the closed door in a tumultuous confusion of emotion, before turning to retrace her steps. Then she halted again.

Philip stood in the parlour doorway, watching her intently. His expression was unreadable, but there was a gravity about it which had not been there a few moments ago. She paused for an instant, returning his gaze in silence, then she ran to him, all tender concern.

'You should not be on your feet,' she said, but as she spoke she was thinking: How long has he been standing there? What did he see?

He turned to put his arm about her as she reached him, and together they went back into the parlour.

CHAPTER
THIRTEEN

As the days lengthened and the snowdrops opened their fragile blossoms in the bare earth beneath the trees Philip slowly regained his strength. Honoria and her aunt vied for the honour of bringing him tempting dishes, ensuring that he had the most comfortable chair and the place closest to the fire, helping the time to pass pleasantly by reading to him from his favourite books. Gradually the colour returned to his face and the cavernous hollows of his cheeks filled out. The haunted look vanished from the depths of his eyes, he was able to walk a little further each day, to eat more heartily and he began to take a more lively interest in the small events of their daily lives. Best of all, Honoria knew, the tranquillity of the countryside and the gentle care of those he loved most in the world did their work of healing. His long ordeal in the Tower became no more than a dark memory, fading quickly so that it had no power even to trouble his dreams. He was home.

Honoria felt that she had never known such happiness as filled her during those first days after his return. She reflected wisely that only when you have known great sorrow can you know true happiness. Her concern to restore Philip to health and strength filled all her days and all her thoughts: it was absorbing and completely satisfying.

Surprisingly, none of them talked very much of the past. It was as if they wanted only to put it behind them, once and for all. It was a cruel nightmare, best forgotten. On the other hand it was some time before they gave any thought to the future either. Having so nearly been parted for ever, Philip and Honoria were content to live for the time being from day to day, simply enjoying the moments as they came.

But it could not last. Inevitably the need to plan for the years ahead crept in to trouble the unruffled serenity of the early days. And so, Honoria found, did thoughts of the past: of Sir Gavin in particular, and that disturbing moment of parting in her uncle's house. She tried very hard to push the memory away when it crept into her consciousness, but she knew it was always there, like a question that was unasked and unanswered, but constantly nagged for her attention.

In the end it was Philip who forced her to confront the memory. It was the first time he had ever deliberately brought up the subject of his ordeal and its consequences, and it happened as they stood together in the doorway one evening, watching the gentle sunset and enjoying the night air, already soft with the coming spring.

'Almost every hour I am reminded how good it is to be alive,' said Philip quietly, after a long silence. Honoria took his hand and squeezed it gently, to signal her agreement. Unbidden into her mind came the thought that if it had been Sir Gavin's hand in hers now she would have felt that electric tingle of delight run through every part of her. I am glad, she thought firmly, that there is nothing of that kind with Philip. Just a quiet contentment in his company.

But when he spoke again his choice of subject startled her by its closeness to her own uncomfortable thoughts.

'I have often wondered about Sir Gavin,' he reflected.

'Yes?' she returned cautiously. Was he about to speak of what he had seen in the hall that day? If he had seen anything, for he had never challenged her with it, or given her any indication that he had witnessed her passionate embrace in the arms of their guest and benefactor.

'I owe him my life, we both know that,' Philip went on. 'When I pressed him on the matter he admitted that he had pleaded with the King when he seemed set against me. I know myself that there was as much evidence against me as against some of those who died, so that there must have been greater weight than usual in my favour to tip the balance as it did. Not only that, but he came in his own coach to bring me home, and then set out to seek for you—but you know about that—' She smiled briefly, but her heart was beating fast wondering what was to come. 'And yet—and yet there was that other unspeakable thing you told me about—the bargain he tried to make with you. I know you gave him nothing, and I know what kind of man he is, or what he is said to be. Yet in spite of all that he had me set free. Why should he do it? What can he have hoped to gain? Or was he simply amazingly generous?'

It was a question she had asked herself so many times that it had almost ceased to have any meaning for her. And she was as far as ever from finding an answer. The only one which seemed to fit was that conscience had overcome him and he had decided at last to make amends for the wrongs he had done her. But some instinct told her that it was too neat and simple a solution, that Sir Gavin's motives were far more complicated than that.

'I don't know,' she replied at last. 'I suppose we can only accept what he did with gratitude and leave it at that.'

A new and horrible thought struck her then, and she stole a sideways glance at Philip. He was gazing out over the dusky garden deep in thought, but without any visible sign of agitation. Even so she was not sure—she watched him for a moment or two longer, then said slowly:

'Philip, you don't think . . . You said you knew . . .'
He turned to look at her in some surprise, and she ended

in a sudden rush of boldness. 'Philip, you don't think, do you, that I gave him what he wanted, and that is why?'

She saw the colour flood his face and knew his answer before he gave it.

'Of course not!' His tone was edged with shock. 'Honoria, how can you think I would even wonder for a moment? No, never. Not for one tiny fraction of a second have I thought that. I have known you almost all my life—I understand that you might have been tempted, faced with the alternative, but that is all.'

She smiled, trembling a little at the violence of his reply. It was as well he did not know how very tempting that shameful offer had been, and how close she had come to yielding to it.

'Thank you for that,' she said, and was glad to see him relax again, her disturbing question forgotten.

'I hear Sir Gavin has bought Silston,' he observed after a moment.

Briefly all her old indignation rose to the surface.

'Yes,' she said, 'and did you hear how he set about it?' He nodded.

'That is exactly why I find it all so puzzling. That a man of his kind—' He smiled suddenly, and shrugged his shoulders. 'Never mind about him, Honoria. See how the snowdrops seem to glow in the dark. I think I like them best of all flowers . . .'

For that evening Sir Gavin ceased to trouble them. But it was only the next day that they spoke of him again. This time Honoria had dressed carefully for a visit to a neighbour who had a new-born son and heir. She had put on the beautiful gloves which Sir Gavin had given her. She thought, regretfully, that they succeeded only in emphasising the general shabbiness of the rest of her clothes, but her other gloves were far too worn for so festive an occasion. Philip noticed them as soon as she joined him in the stable yard.

'You're very fine today,' he commented. 'Where did those come from?'

She was angry to find herself blushing.

'From Sir Gavin,' she replied, as casually as she could. She thought she saw him stiffen a little.

'Indeed!' he said. 'When was that?'

She told him, trying to cover her confusion with a calmness of manner. After all, she had nothing to hide. They were a gift, and that was all. But she knew Philip was watching her intently as she spoke.

'You seem to have seen rather more of Sir Gavin than I thought,' he commented when she had come to an end. He was frowning a little, and she felt her heart quicken uncomfortably. Was he suspicious of her behaviour after all? In the end, as they set out on their journey, she drew a deep breath and told him the whole story, as calmly and accurately as she could. It seemed the only way to keep him from thinking ill of her.

When she had finished he nodded, and said: 'I see,' then made no further comment. She was not sure if that meant that he regarded the whole matter as too trivial to be worthy of discussion, or if he was too distressed to speak of it. She had never before been so uncertain of Philip's attitude towards her, and she did not like the sensation. She felt that for the first time in all the years they had known each other their close companionship was threatened. She wanted to challenge him to say what he was thinking, but he began to talk of something else and the opportunity was lost.

As time passed she longed to recapture the tranquil happiness of the days just after his return home. But that seemed to have gone for ever, taking with it even the easy everyday contentment of their life together before his arrest. She began to think that in some strange indefinable way she had lost him, that he was estranged from her, beyond her reach. She feared it had something to do with what she had told him of Sir Gavin, but she could not be sure. After all, that was over now, a thing of the past. She would never see Sir Gavin again, except in the distance as he hunted over his estates; and she would be careful to avoid the vicinity of Silston as far as possible.

Whatever the explanation she knew that Philip had changed. He seemed to be restless, given to long walks alone, sometimes at night or in the pouring rain, when he was apparently oblivious of his surroundings. He was often deeply preoccupied, lost in sombre thoughts so far removed from her and his stepmother that it was difficult to make him hear when a meal was ready or there was something to be discussed. Honoria longed to ask him what was on his mind, but she sensed that it would be an intrusion, that he could only talk to her if and when he chose.

His restlessness seemed to have infected her, too. She could not settle for long to her sewing or her reading or to the many household tasks without longing soon to be somewhere else, pacing her room, gazing out of her window, wandering in the garden.

In the end Aunt Anne could not help but notice the disconcerting unsettled state which was afflicting both her niece and her stepson.

'You can't sit still for five minutes together these days,' she said to Honoria one day, as their methodical mending of worn bedlinen was interrupted yet again by Honoria's need to go to the window and gaze out at the garden, sparkling after a sudden shower. 'Philip's been home two months now: it's nearly April—don't you think it's time you thought of marriage?'

Honoria stood transfixed, her arms tense at her sides. Marriage. It was as if she had never thought of it before. Yet had it not always been there, the welcoming goal towards which they worked, the inevitable joyful conclusion to a lifetime of deep affection?

She shivered suddenly. All at once it seemed to have

turned cold. She left the window and came slowly back to the fireside, her head bent.

They should have been married by now, if it had not been for the events of last November. She had always supposed that she would become Philip's wife as soon as he was free. And yet she had scarcely given it a thought since she returned home. It came to her now as something new and strange.

She raised her head and her eyes met Aunt Anne's, shrewd and thoughtful.

'Perhaps you'd better talk to Philip about it,' suggested her aunt quietly.

Has she guessed my thoughts? wondered Honoria. But since she was not quite sure herself exactly what she was thinking that seemed unlikely.

It was sensible advice that she should talk to Philip, but not so easily carried out. He was absent for most of the day on one of his interminable walks, and when he did return, cloak drenched and mud-spattered to the knees, he shut himself in his room for the rest of the evening and would not even emerge for supper. Honoria and her aunt exchanged troubled glances across the table, but made no comment. It was a silent and uncomfortable meal.

The next day Philip went out before the household was up, taking a crust of bread from the crock for his breakfast and leaving no word as to where he had gone, which was not in itself unusual, but this time Honoria bit her lip to check the tears when she realised what had happened.

She sensed that he had reached some crisis at last. But if only he would talk to her about it! The hours dragged interminably that day as they waited for his return, and began towards evening to fear that he might not come back at all.

He came home finally at dusk, grey with exhaustion. Honoria met him in the hall and gave a cry of dismay at his condition, but he brushed her aside and went wearily up to his room and closed the door.

They had supper late, and to Honoria's relief he joined them for it, washed and changed and abruptly transformed from the desperate figure who had passed her an hour ago. His expression was grave enough, but he made an attempt at conversation and even, once, ventured a little joke, which delighted both women so much that they laughed far more than it deserved. But still he gave no explanation for his strange behaviour.

And then when Anne Blount had bidden them goodnight and gone upstairs to bed he took hold of Honoria's arm as she turned to follow her aunt.

'Wait!' he commanded in a low voice. 'I want to speak with you.'

She retraced her steps and sat down again in her seat by the fire, waiting in silence for him to begin. Her heart quickened with apprehension. What was he going to say after all this time?

For several minutes he said nothing at all, but simply stood a little way off, looking at her with a frown, as if he did not know how to begin. At last he said:

'Honoria, I saw Father Swayne today.'

The colour rushed to her face: he must want to speak to her about their marriage. The frantic beating of her heart seemed almost to stifle her.

'Oh?' she said breathlessly.

'Yes,' he said. 'He's staying at Sir Marmaduke Selby's house at present.'

The statement drove all thought of impending marriage from her head.

'But that's nearly twenty miles away! Oh, Philip, no wonder you were tired. But . . .' She hesitated now, though she thought she knew what his answer would be. 'Was it necessary to go so far?'

'Very necessary,' he said. Another little silence followed, and then he added: 'Honoria, he asked about our plans to be married—among other things.'

'And what did you tell him?' she asked.

He came closer, and sat down in his customary chair, facing her across the hearth.

'I . . . we talked a great deal—but not much about that.'

She watched him as he bent his head, frowning deeply as if he found it difficult to continue.

'About what then?' she asked, after yet another pause.

At last he raised his head and leaned back in the chair, his eyes meeting hers with a new directness, the words suddenly released.

'Honoria, when I was in the Tower I had a great deal of time for reflection—more, perhaps, than I wanted,' he put in wryly. 'Maybe it is good sometimes to be forced to look at things as closely as that—to stare death in the face and learn to know yourself in the cold light of that experience. I know I have felt since that there must have been a purpose in it all, that I was being tested for something—but I'll come to that in a moment.

'One thought which was constantly with me was of you. I'm sure you will realise that, knowing what we mean to each other. And—' he hesitated, and then went on: 'Honoria, I find this very hard to say, because I am not sure how you will take it. You must believe that I feel I must say it, to be fair to us both—'

'Go on,' she prompted gently.

'I feel now, after long thought, that it would be wrong for us to marry.'

She gasped: it was the very last thing she had expected him to say.

'Wrong! But, Philip, why?'

He smiled faintly.

'I think it would be almost like a brother wedding a sister for me to marry you.'

'But we are not blood relations!' she protested.

'That's not what I meant,' he said. 'Oh, I know we love each other deeply, and always will. But it is the quiet companionable enduring love of a brother for a sister—or at least that is what I feel—I can't speak for you, of course. It is not, to me, the kind of love of which good marriages are made.'

'But that's nonsense!' she exclaimed. 'Few marriages achieve anything even as good as that.'

His eyes were troubled now.

'I had hoped you would feel as I do,' he said. 'That what we have between us is good and true and enduring, but that it is not enough, just as it is. Tell me,' he asked earnestly, 'do you really, deeply, in your heart, want to be my wife?'

She searched desperately for an answer, as his eyes were searching hers, but none came. Or none clear enough to help him now.

'I . . . I don't know,' she faltered.

'I think perhaps you do know if you think about it long enough. I think you know that our love for each other is not meant for marriage, because there is another man who has your heart.'

The colour sprang fiery red to her face.

'What do you mean?' she demanded sharply.

'You know what I mean, Honoria. I saw you in Sir Gavin's arms in London.'

So he had seen, and drawn the worst possible conclusion.

'No!' she exclaimed. 'You're quite wrong. That was not my doing.'

He gave a lop-sided smile.

'No? You did not seem to be resisting very effectively.'

She would not have thought her colour could deepen as it did.

'I hope I know the difference between love and lust,' she retorted stiffly.

'So do I,' he agreed. 'But it was not lust which brought that look to your eyes when you spoke of him to me the other day.'

'That was indignation,' she objected. 'I told you the dreadful things he did.'

'And how you wounded him, and how deeply it troubled you,' he reminded her. 'No, Honoria, that won't do.'

She swept to her feet and crossed to the curtained window, suddenly angry.

'You are jealous, Philip: that's what it is. There can be no other explanation. How can you think me so weak as to care for a man like that?'

'I don't think love follows the rules,' he said peaceably. 'But never mind. It is not worth arguing over—because I think that even if you had never set eyes on Sir Gavin it would still be wrong for us to marry. Come and sit down again.' He waited until she had obeyed, and then went on: 'Perhaps I'm being selfish, but I think not—I don't want to hurt you . . .'

'It is not because of what you think I feel that you're saying this,' she said, the hurt showing in her eyes, 'but because you no longer wish to marry me.'

'I don't wish to marry at all,' he said. 'I think I have always known it somewhere inside myself, but until I was in prison I never recognised it.'

Fear twisted deep within her as some instinct born of her understanding of him told her what he meant to do.

'Then what do you want?' she asked in a whisper, though she knew what his answer would be.

'I want to go away—right away, that is, across the sea. And think a great deal more. And then, if I'm still of the same mind, I shall become a priest.'

This time there was a long silence. Honoria thought of the midnight knock on the door, the searchers turning the house to chaos, the airless hiding place which was never wholly finally safe, the fever-ridden prison, the scaffold: and she shivered. Had he escaped so narrowly with his life for this? But she knew the thought must be left unspoken. All she said was:

'What of Aunt Anne?'

That, at least, troubled him, for she read it in his sudden frown.

'I hope she will understand,' he said. 'But we shall have to see.' And his eyes thanked her for her own understanding.

Honoria feared for Anne Blount, so frail in health now, so completely devoted to her stepson, so deeply happy to have him safe. She wondered if Philip would give up his plans if the old woman asked it of him.

But she did not ask. She surprised them both by her calm acceptance of what he told her, as if she had expected it all along and knew it was right. She even made Honoria a little ashamed of her own doubts.

Three weeks later in the darkness before dawn Philip left the Manor House. They watched him go, a darker shadow in the lane trudging towards the unseen dawn, and Honoria knew it would be long years before they could hope to see him again.

Beside her, Anne Blount sobbed once, a sharp broken sound in the night, and her hand clasped Honoria's in a painful grip. Then she said, quite calmly: 'I shall never see him again,' and they turned and went into the house.

CHAPTER
FOURTEEN

A GENTLE shimmer of green covered the trees and hedgerows, and the new grass was patterned with violets and primroses: somewhere a cuckoo called.

Sir Gavin viewed it all without enthusiasm, and wished heartily that he was in London. Next week, perhaps, he would go back, if Lady Philomena would allow him to stray from her side at last. She wanted his advice, she had said, concerning some matter to do with her estates, only he could help her. But when he arrived at Belfield he had found that there was after all nothing of any importance requiring his attention. It was quite obvious that Lady Philomena had wanted some excuse to make him come running at her beck and call. Perhaps it gave her a comforting sense of power or perhaps she thought there might be other temptations in London to lure him into unfaithfulness while she was away. Whatever the reason, she had brought him down to Belfield on a wild-goose chase and now turned sulky and unpleasant whenever he spoke of leaving. He did not want to quarrel with her yet. They were to be married at the end of the summer: time enough then to show her who was master. So he stayed, and was thoroughly bored. He wanted congenial company to pass the time, someone pleasant to talk to, but he might have been in the desert for all the companionship he found. He had wandered out into the garden now to escape from the long-winded tedium of his betrothed's conversation.

He had been to Silston once since he came here, just to make sure that everything was progressing well with the furnishing and redecorating. He looked on his property there as a place of escape once he was married. At Silston he would be able to entertain whomsoever he chose, while his wife dozed over her sermons at Belfield, waiting for him to pay her an occasional dutiful visit.

But he did not want to go to Silston again, it was too close to Lower Kilworth. And it was too soon, he felt, to venture so near to Honoria's house. When a couple married for love it took a long time for the first shine to wear off. Later, she would be more vulnerable.

He decided, nevertheless, to order his horse to be saddled and go for a ride. And almost without knowing it he found himself taking the road that led past Silston and on to Lower Kilworth. He shrugged resignedly: very likely he would not see her. And if he did—then perhaps he could turn it to his advantage. He had, after all, completely bungled his last meeting with Honoria. To this day he did not know why he had behaved in so sulky and irritable a manner on that occasion. He had planned it all so carefully, too: the distant unconcerned politeness, the off-hand charm, the air of courteous sympathy for her and for Philip. And instead some demon had got into him and made him sharp-tongued and awkward, and then driven him to that final moment of uncontrolled desire in the hall—he reddened to think of it. He tried to put it out of his mind, and rode on, deep in thought.

And then he saw her. He had just passed a farm, scarcely heeding the dogs that ran barking behind him, and then the lane curved round, skirting a field which led across to a little wood. There, climbing over a stile at the far side of the field, was Honoria. It was a moment before he recognised her, so absurdly young and girlish did she look. She wore a simple gown of faded green, and her lovely hair hung loose about her, bound only by a bright green ribbon tied at the nape of her neck. She carried a basket, and looked more like a simple country girl than the respectable gentlewoman he knew her to be. She crossed the field and followed a path along its further edge until she was lost to sight in the wood.

Marriage suits her, he thought, with a pang of regret. The sensible thing, now, was to turn round and ride back to Belfield and give her a few more weeks or even months to realise that Philip was not everything. But he found he was not in the mood to be sensible. Instead he put his horse to the hedge, to leap it lightly and easily, and cantered across the field towards the wood.

The trees were mostly young beech and oak, and their branches low. He was forced to dismount and follow the path through them on foot, leading his horse. He had lost sight of her now, and he was afraid he might never find her, for he could not be sure she had come this way. Many smaller paths curved away to right and left through the trees, and she might have taken any one of them.

The path began to travel gradually uphill, and then topped a rise before running down again into a little valley, where more mature trees sheltered a grassy bank beside a little stream. The light caught on something moving there, something of a softer green than the sparkling new growth in the wood, and then on the warm fire-colour of Honoria's hair as she bent to gather primroses and lay them in her basket.

Sir Gavin stood quite still, watching her, his heart beating fast. She came slowly nearer to where he was, patterned by the light and shade of the wood. The slender curves of her body moved with a lovely liquid grace, more marked in that simple gown than in the stiff lines of the black velvet in which he had seen her last. Her hair shone as it fell about her shoulders, the colours changing when she stooped or rose again from gold to bronze and brown, and then to copper and chestnut and every shade between. She was like some silent spirit of the wood, slipping soft-footed over the grass.

As quietly as he could he tethered his horse to a low

branch and went towards her. She did not know he was there until he was a yard or two away, and she gave a little startled cry as he removed his hat and bowed.

He realised then that he had been wrong about one thing. At a distance she looked as young and carefree as a girl of sixteen: close to, the bruised shadows were only too clear beneath her eyes, and the pallor brought on by too many sleepless nights. So marriage did not suit her after all! His heart leapt triumphantly. He had been right to force this meeting on her before she had grown accustomed to the deficiencies of her husband. Later, perhaps, she would come to accept that he could not give her all she hoped to find. Satisfaction gave a new sparkle to his eyes.

'Good day, Mistress Honoria,' he said. He could not quite bring himself to address her by her new name, as Mistress Blount.

Her face was not pale now, but coloured like a wild rose, and she was breathing quickly, her eyes wide. He thought inconsequentially that they were like the spring-time woods, in their myriad shades of green and blue and brown, the colours of leaf and stem and earth and water.

'Good day, sir,' she replied, rather unsteadily. 'I . . . I had not expected . . .' She broke off, as if she did not quite know what to say. He wondered if she was remembering their last meeting, and was embarrassed by the recollection. He smiled charmingly, to put her at her ease.

'You're like the spirit of spring today,' he said. 'But why are you robbing the wood of those poor primroses?'

She gave a reluctant smile in answer to his cheerful question.

'They are for a lotion my aunt likes to make,' she explained. 'But she is growing a little too old to gather them herself. For best results they should be picked at dawn, but—' again she broke off.

'But you were too much the slug-abed today,' he finished for her. He felt a twinge of jealousy thinking of what might have kept her in bed so late. Damn Master Blount!

'How is your aunt?' he went on. 'And your—and Master Blount?'

'Well enough, as far as I could tell when I left the house this morning,' she replied rather stiffly, half-turning away from him to a nearby clump of primroses. Something in her manner puzzled him. It might be accounted for simply by embarrassment, but he sensed rather that she was concealing something. Still, if her new marriage had already proved unhappy, she was not likely to want anyone outside the immediate family to know.

He stood watching her for a moment as her slender fingers moved among the flowers, picking carefully—a few here, a few there—so that it was not too obvious that they had gone. Then his eyes wandered over the sunny clearing, trying to find something that might interest her.

'Is that a little waterfall in the stream down there?' he asked at last.

She straightened, and followed his gaze.

'A very small one,' she said discouragingly.

'I'm going down,' he decided, and called over his shoulder: 'Come—'

She left her basket where it lay by his discarded hat and followed him, more slowly. She was, in any case, tiring a little of her task.

'I didn't know you cared for the countryside,' she observed with a note of disbelief. 'Except to hunt over it, of course.'

'Ah, but that depends on the company,' he returned, reflecting how entirely true that was. He tried to imagine Lady Philomena standing in Honoria's place at his side, and the very thought filled him with tedium.

He reached the foot of the slope and paused at the edge of the stream, beside the miniature rock-fall over which the water danced with a tiny sparkling curve. He smiled at her as she joined him: it was a warming smile, unexpectedly companionable.

'I remember spending hours damming streams such as this when I was a boy. Did you do that too?'

So his childhood had not all been grim poverty, she thought. He had crouched down now, his strong brown hands gathering pebbles and setting them to form a barrier across the stream.

'The water always seems to get through somehow,' he commented. 'Though once I can remember stopping a burn altogether. Only it came on to thunder and I had to seek shelter, and when I came back the water was a brown torrent and my poor little dam had gone for good.'

He grinned up at her, and she smiled at the spectacle of this great man, in his velvet cloak and embroidered doublet, absorbed in such a childish activity. He leaned over the water again and she gazed down at his bent head, observing the way the thickly waving hair, as richly golden brown as a cornfield in August, sprang into glossy curls at the ends, just above the lace-edged crispness of his little ruff. She felt again the strange turning sensation in the pit of her stomach which she had come to associate with him.

He completed his dam in silence, then rose to his feet, shaking the moisture from his fingers.

'A good morning's work,' he said; 'I shall take a well-earned rest.'

The bank where they stood was mossy and warmed by the sun, and he stretched himself on it, his hands linked behind his head. Honoria sat down near him, resting her chin on updrawn knees.

'Now if I had brought some food this would be paradise indeed,' he said, gazing up at the sky. To

Honoria it seemed as if its dazzling blue was exactly reflected in his eyes.

'Why is it that men always seem to be thinking of food?' she asked, half laughing.

'There speaks the little housewife,' he said with a slight edge to his voice. For that moment she had sounded too much the happy bride for his comfort. 'But you wrong me,' he added more warmly. 'Even without food I would not be at Court now for all the gold in Spain.'

'That I find very hard to believe,' she said.

He sat up then with a sudden laugh, and propped himself on one elbow, facing her.

'I must tell you about a masque that was given two weeks ago before the King—' He went on to tell her a long and hilarious tale involving court ladies dressed as nymphs and shepherdesses in diaphanous draperies tripping and stumbling half-drunk through their parts, of elaborate scenery which collapsed and mechanical devices which failed to work, of a cupid who lost his wig and of so many other disasters that she could never remember the details afterwards. The story bore out her conviction that the court was decadent in the extreme, but he told it so well, and with such vivid detail, and such an infectious sparkle in his blue eyes that she could not help but be amused. All the last traces of strain slid from her and she laughed delightedly, a low gurgling throaty laugh of sheer pleasure which took him completely by surprise.

He turned to gaze at her face, alive and glowing with laughter, then he drew in his breath sharply and reached out a hand to touch her cheek.

'Och, wee lassie, but you're beautiful,' he whispered.

Her eyes were full of merriment as she returned his gaze.

'You're very Scots all of a sudden,' she said. Her voice shook a little at the emotion in his eyes, and the laughter slowly faded from her own. For a moment neither of them moved. Then his hand traced its way down her cheek to her throat, and round to the nape of her neck, drawing her towards him. Just for an instant she saw his eyes, intensely blue, gazing deep into hers, then his arms went about her and drew her down onto the grass to lie beside him.

'Oh, Honoria,' he murmured, and his mouth moved to the silken warmth of her throat, and then on down, his hands tugging at the lacing of her bodice. She did not even begin to resist. There in the warm spring sunlight, with the sounds of stream and birdsong in her ears, the sweet grass beneath and his arms about her, she knew there was nothing she wanted more than this. She threw back her head and closed her eyes and thrust longing fingers into the thickness of his hair, and gave herself up to ecstasy.

But somewhere within Sir Gavin the cool head which had rarely failed him and had brought him against the odds to the dizzy heights of the King's favour: that carefully calculating part of him struck a warning note, and he drew away from her just in time. He turned on to his back, breathing fast, and slid those sensitive hands beneath his head, as if they were safer held there. Then he said lightly:

'I'll wager Philip never kissed you like that.'

She drew a sharp breath which was almost a sob.

'Philip is a good man!' she said, the more harshly because her whole body cried out for him to take her in his arms again.

'Ah, but good men make very tedious husbands,' he returned, in something approaching his usual casual tones. She gazed at him in astonishment, trying through the painful breathlessness of half-satisfied desire to understand what he was implying. He turned on to his elbow again to face her, but at a safe distance this time.

'Admit it, Honoria: your marriage is not what you

hoped it would be. If it were you'd not have allowed me to kiss you like that just now—or wanted it of me.'

Honoria stared at him. Slowly, at last, all the ill-assorted pieces fell into place. So that was it! That was why he had changed so suddenly, sending her those pretty gloves, freeing Philip: he had hoped to lull her into a sense of security and trust, to let her go away and marry and try to forget him. And then he had planned to come, exactly as he had done today, to console her for a marriage that was less than satisfying. Only he had miscalculated, for she was not married, and he did not know it. She felt a quiver of angry triumph, and sat up, her back very straight,

'Why did you not take me then, if that's what you think?' she demanded, her eyes suddenly diamond hard. The look in them disconcerted him a little, but he replied amiably:

'Because you would without doubt have slapped my face afterwards and walked away without another word, the picture of outraged virtue. And you would very likely have confessed it all to Philip, and vowed never to lay yourself open to temptation again. And then I should never have seen you again. But I was rather hoping we might meet from time to time and that you might come to want what I can offer you. Philip need never know, but you might even be happier with him because of me.' He thought fleetingly of Silston, with Honoria there, a frequent guest. And then he noticed the hard line of her mouth and knew with a sinking of the heart that he had lost again.

'You are despicable!' she exclaimed, and scrambled to her feet. She stood looking down at him, her eyes blazing. 'How after all this time you can still believe me capable of that I do not know. I was a fool just now. I thought perhaps you cared for me a little, and allowed you more freedom than I ought. But you can be quite sure that I shall never again in all my life allow you to lay one finger on me. Now I am going home. I hope we shall never meet again.' She turned and began to make her way quickly up the slope to where she had left her basket.

Sir Gavin sprang to his feet and ran after her.

'Honoria! Come here!' He caught up with her and grasped her arm, but she shook him off angrily. 'Listen to me!'

She did stop then, and turned to face him, but he knew she would walk away at once if she did not like what he said.

'Honoria, don't take that high moral tone with me! Can you deny that a few minutes ago you would have been unfaithful to Philip without a moment's hesitation?'

He waited for her to blush, to look disconcerted, but instead there was an unmistakable gleam of satisfaction in her eyes.

'Yes, I can deny it,' she said. 'I am not married to Philip.'

He gazed at her in astonishment.

'Not married to him? What do you mean . . . ? You mean you are not *yet* married to him?'

'I am not married to him, and I am not going to be married to him. We agreed that it was better so, and he has gone away.' As she spoke she recognised for the first time that she had accepted Philip's decision without bitterness or regret. She missed him, of course, and always would, but she knew now that he had made the right choice for both of them.

She returned from her reflections to the realisation that Sir Gavin had turned pale and was looking at her with an odd light in his eyes. Amazement was there, but also some deeper emotion she could not read. He was silent for a long time, and then he said suddenly:

'Marry me, Honoria.'

She gasped, then she realised that he was as

astonished as she at the words. *Dear God, what have I done?* said his eyes. There was a stunned silence, and then the colour slowly flooded his face, and Honoria said quietly:

'I don't think you meant that.'

He put an unsteady hand to his forehead, as if he were slightly dazed.

'No . . .' he admitted. 'No, I don't think I did. I am sorry . . . I don't know why . . .'

'You are betrothed to the Lady Philomena,' Honoria reminded him, as if he were suffering from loss of memory, 'and I am a poor Catholic gentlewoman who can offer you nothing, least of all,' she added severely, 'what you seem to want from me most.'

So much so, she thought to herself, that you find yourself proposing marriage when all else fails. But she did not feel it would help matters to say it out loud. She felt very uncomfortable as it was, standing there under his bewildered gaze.

'Yes,' he said slowly. 'Yes, I see that now.' He stooped to pick up his hat, and then gave a slight bow. 'We shan't meet again, Mistress Somervell, I can promise you that. Good day.'

She watched as he walked away from her up the slope to where his horse was tethered, and she continued to stand there as he untied the horse and mounted and rode away without once looking back. Then she shivered, and glanced up to see if a cloud had covered the sun, but it shone as brightly as ever, though all the golden light seemed to have gone from the wood.

Slowly, surely, irrevocably, a new realisation formed within her and lay heavy as lead on her heart. Philip had been right. She loved Sir Gavin Hamilton, and she had just sent him away, out of her life for ever.

CHAPTER
FIFTEEN

Sɪʀ Gavin returned to London the next day in a furious rage at his own incompetence. What on earth had happened to him in the wood yesterday that he should have lost his touch so disastrously, just when he needed it most? Now he had lost her for ever. He had not even had the short-lived satisfaction of seducing her, thinking misguidedly as he had that he was going to gain some more permanent pleasure. At least if he had taken her once that would have been better than nothing. As it was, he was going to have to accept that he was left with nothing, and could hope for nothing. Honoria Somervell was not for him.

He threw himself with desperate enthusiasm into the pleasures of the Court: balls, masques, visits to the play-house, eating and drinking, hunting and cock-fighting. And women: women of all kinds, from married court ladies with complaisant husbands to the fashionable city courtesans in their scented lodgings. After all, what was Honoria but a woman?—and one woman was as good as another for what he wanted.

He was thankful at least that she had been quick to prevent him from making matters worse there in the wood. He blushed for shame whenever he thought of the unaccountable impulse which had led him to propose to her. Even if he had been free she was no bride for a man seeking to keep his place in the world: a poverty-stricken Catholic with doubtful connections—he could hardly do worse. And he was not, thank goodness, free at all. At the end of August he would be joined for ever to the Lady Philomena at a splendid marriage ceremony before the King. James loved to spend lavishly on such occasions, and there would be masques and banquets and magnificent clothes and jewels and gifts, and the King would come to their room the next morning and sit on their bed and ask how the wedding night had gone. Sir Gavin did not greatly care for that last peculiarity of the King's, but it was to be endured for the sake of pleasing him.

Early in August Lady Philomena returned to London from Belfield to assist in the final preparations for the marriage. She had now, Gavin noticed, developed an unappealingly self-satisfied expression at the prospect before her. It lit her face whenever he paid her the least attention. You wait, my lady, he thought when he saw it: once we are wed I'll wipe that look from your face. But for now he was meticulously attentive—when he had nothing better to do—bringing her gifts, cultivating an appearance of avid interest whenever she spoke to him, encouraging her to believe that the prospect of their marriage filled him with boundless delight. Which, he thought, it did, in a sense, for with her as his wife he would have climbed almost to the summit of his power. A peerage next perhaps—he could not go a great deal further. It was a satisfying thought.

But for all that he was not satisfied. Though he filled every spare moment with an exhausting round of pleasure he was still, underneath it all, achingly bored. It was like eating the same splendid dish, day after day: in time it came to seem stale and tasteless. And yet he varied his women and his other activities as much as he could. In the end he found that the most satisfactory solution was to take the edge off his boredom with drink: seen through a haze of alcohol life was not quite so unbearable.

He was almost sober, however, when he returned home from the bed of his most recent mistress, one morning just after daybreak. The pleasant drunkenness of last night had worn off during the past hours, and he was anxious to return to that happy state as soon as possible. It was a fine morning, and on impulse he had sent his coach home without him and decided to walk the short distance to his house. But he was beginning to regret that decision now. His head was aching, despite the fresh air, and he thought longingly of the good Canary wine awaiting his attention in the library.

There were not many people about as yet, although some careful housewives were already on their way to market. Turning a corner he almost fell over a ragged boy, curled up asleep in a doorway, and was sharply reminded of his own early years, when a satin doublet and rings on his fingers and the King's favour would have seemed a remote and impossible dream. Rather to his own surprise he felt in his purse and drew out a coin and slid it under the boy's outstretched hand, where he would find it when he awoke. Then, a little ashamed of his impulse, he glanced quickly round to make sure that he had not been observed.

There was no one about, he saw with relief. Then he stood still, suddenly alert. A man came into sight around the corner he had just passed: a light-haired, pock-marked man, burly and roughly dressed. Surely that was the man Honoria had asked him about, as they left Whitehall that day in January?

He came a little way along the street, then turned into an alley between two houses. Gavin watched for a moment longer, but he did not reappear. He shrugged his shoulders and walked on slowly: clearly the man was of no importance. Even so, he glanced behind him one last time before he left the street.

Further on, where the roads were more crowded, some instinct made him turn again. And this time he glimpsed the bleached hair moving rapidly through the crowd. After that he looked round often, and always the man was there somewhere in the throng. Once he seemed to be casting a casual eye over a market stall, once he paused to gaze into a shop window, once he slipped into a baker's to buy a loaf.

Gavin quickened his pace and on impulse took a short cut through a narrow lane known to few who did not live in the area. But when he looked behind him again on rejoining the main thoroughfare the man was still there. He felt a swift surge of anger. How dared anyone set a spy on him! He was almost tempted to go back and challenge the man, to take him by the throat and shake him until he admitted who paid him. But if he refused to tell then Gavin might never know the answer.

Coming within sight of his house he saw Sim hovering close by, an anxious look upon his face. Gavin called to him, and he came over, clearly relieved. Before he could speak Gavin said quickly:

'Don't look round, Sim, but there's a man following me. He may hang about and keep watch on the house now, I don't know, but when he goes I want you to go after him. Don't let him see you, but let me know who pays him, if you can.'

'Has he got white hair and pock marks?' asked Sim.

'You've seen him too, then?' said Gavin in surprise. Sim nodded.

'He's been waiting around here once or twice lately—and before that, too. I've kept half an eye on him, but I wasn't sure if he was keeping watch or not.' He ran a casual glance over the passing throng. 'Yes, I can see him now. He's across there, trying to look as if he wasn't interested. He's moving away now, slowly—'

'Follow him, Sim. And bring me word as soon as you can.'

'Yes, sir—' He hesitated. 'One thing, sir—'

'Quick, there's no time—he's just gone round that corner—after him!'

Sim tried to speak again, but Gavin passed him quickly and disappeared into the house. The man

shrugged, and set out on his errand. He came within
sight of the pock-marked man again at the corner, and
made his discreet way through the crowd behind him,
unobserved.

Gavin stepped into the hall of his house and there,
abruptly, stood still. Behind him he heard the sound of
the door closing. He glanced round and saw, in place of
the expected servant in his own livery, a soldier in the
King's colours.

He turned back and looked about him. The hall was
full of soldiers, watching him. With them was the
sprucely-dressed courtier who had summoned Honoria
to the King. Gavin felt a sudden lurch of fear, but his
expression held only anger.

'What is the meaning of this intrusion?' he demanded.

The courtier approached and bowed with deep
respect. Gavin noted with satisfaction that he was clearly
nervous. It was no small thing to be ordered to in-
vade the royal favourite's house with an armed band of
men.

'His Majesty the King commands that you wait upon
him at once,' he said, the force of the words rather
undermined by his apprehensive tone. 'I was sent last
night, but you were not to be found—' he added.

Gavin walked past him and began to mount the stairs.

'His Majesty knows that he has only to say the word
and I will be there,' he replied haughtily. 'There was no
need for this—' He waved a disdainful hand towards the
soldiers.

Alarmed, the courtier ran agitatedly after him,
following him halfway up the stairs.

'Sir Gavin, I must protest—you must come—'

Gavin paused and turned to look down at him.

'Surely I may be permitted to change into something
more appropriate to the King's presence?' he asked, his
eyebrows faintly raised.

'The King commanded that you come at once, sir,' faltered the messenger.

'Since you have waited all night I hardly think another half hour can make much difference,' returned Gavin, and went on his way.

He was tempted to go first to the library and try to recapture the comforting numbness of last night: it was a good wine, and strong. But it occurred to him that he might need all his wits about him through the coming hours. If he had to fight to keep his hold on the King . . .

Reluctantly he turned in the opposite direction and went to his room. John waited there, ready to help him dress. He must choose his clothes with the greatest possible care. He stood just inside the door, frowning with concentration over the problem.

'The blue and silver, sir?' suggested John tentatively. Gavin smiled.

'Yes, John, that's the one.'

Tenderly John lifted it from the clothes press, and then came to help his master out of the crushed satin of last night.

Looking at himself in his new and expensive mirror Sir Gavin was sure he had been right. The doublet was of silk, the warm summer blue of cornflowers, delicately and intricately embroidered with silver thread, and sewn with pearls. Hose of the same colour went with it, and white silk stockings. Blue and silver shoes and a long French cloak of silver grey velvet draped casually about him completed the ensemble. The colour seemed to emphasise the brilliant blue of his eyes, the tanned complexion, the corn-gold of his hair.

He took the broad-brimmed grey hat and embroidered gloves in his hand and set off, slowly, along the gallery and down the stairs. To the men waiting in the hall he looked magnificent: cool, aloof, dazzlingly handsome. There was no trace in his manner of a man in fear for his position or his life.

'Well, gentlemen, shall we go?' he asked as he reached the hall. The courtier came forward to meet him.

'I am afraid,' he said apologetically, 'that I must ask for your sword—the King's orders, sir.'

That did anger Sir Gavin, but he could not risk the indignity of an argument. Frowning, he unbuckled the fine sword in its silver sheath and handed it in silence to the courtier.

Then the soldiers fell into line to form an escort to take him to the King.

King James waited for his favourite in the small untidy study he used sometimes, deep in the warren of rooms and passages which was the Palace of Whitehall. Gavin was relieved to find that they were to be alone together, but the King's expression as he came in was not reassuring. His eyes were cold and unwelcoming, and he did not stir from his fringed and cushioned chair at the far side of a book-littered table, nor did he invite Sir Gavin to be seated, as once he would have done.

Gavin bowed and ventured a smile, but there was no answering warmth in the King's eyes.

'You should have known, sire,' he said, 'that there was no need to send such a train to bring me to you. I am always ready at your command.'

The King frowned, stretching his arms across the table in front of him.

'Are you so, sir? I was not sure that I could rely on that any longer.'

'You can have no reason to think otherwise, sire,' returned Sir Gavin. 'When have I done anything to give you reason to doubt me?'

'Should I not doubt when you give aid and comfort to my enemies?' demanded the King.

Gavin felt the colour drain from his face. What had they found against him? He did not think he had ever laid himself open to accusations of disloyalty or treason. But a determined enemy could do great harm with very little evidence. And he had many enemies.

'I do not understand you, sire,' he said guardedly.

'Do you not indeed? What of the man Philip Blount? What do you have to say about him?'

Gavin gazed at the King in bewilderment. What had Philip Blount to do with him now? That episode was long over and done with.

'Your Majesty in your great mercy had him released from the Tower, sire—' he began.

'At your instigation,' the King reminded him. 'You were most pressing, I remember. You protested that you were sure of his loyalty, that I should never have cause for regret were I to show mercy. Have you forgotten that?'

'No, sire, indeed not,' said Gavin. 'And I have no reason to think I misjudged the matter.'

'No reason, when the man has gone overseas and is without doubt plotting the overthrow of this Kingdom with other malcontents who escaped my judgement last November?'

Gavin's heart beat uncomfortably fast. He remembered now that Honoria had told him her cousin had left home. Damn Philip Blount! After all he had done for him, why did he have to leave the country like that? Surely he must have known how suspicious it would look? Why in God's name, thought Gavin harshly, did I ever get myself entangled in this affair in the first place? Damn Honoria Somervell for her lovely eyes and her sweet lips and—

He realised that the King was watching him with those penetrating eyes, and was brought abruptly back to the present. He knew what threatened him now, and he knew the extent of his danger. At the worst, it could lead to a charge of high treason, at best to the loss of the King's favour. If he allowed it to do so—

He dropped suddenly onto one knee, his eyes, very blue under the dark lashes, gazing up at the King's sombre face.

'Your Majesty,' he said earnestly, his voice warm with emotion, 'I begged for Master Blount's life at your hands because I believed most sincerely that he was innocent of any malice against your person. To my knowledge he is so still, though I have not seen him since the day he left the Tower. Never, never in all my life have I acted with disloyalty towards you. You are my King, sire, and your life and well-being are, to me, as my own: sacred, to be preserved and cherished at all costs.'

The King was silent for a moment, then he said with an unexpectedly wistful note:

'I would believe you loyal, my Gavin, if I could—'

'Then believe it, sire,' implored Gavin, 'for it is true.'

The King came round the table and stood looking down at him.

'Get up, man, get up,' he said impatiently.

Gavin rose to his feet with a surge of renewed hope. At least that alarming coldness had gone from the King's manner.

'Tell me,' King James went on, 'what was the man Philip Blount to you? Or, rather, the woman who was to wed him—that bonny little gentlewoman who came to Court—what part did she play in all this?'

'She came to ask my favour on behalf of her cousin,' replied Gavin. 'That's all.' He was annoyed to feel his colour rising under the King's shrewd gaze.

'That was all, was it?' said the King. Gavin wondered with alarm what else he had heard. 'Did you not see her many times, before Blount's release—and afterwards too?'

'Yes,' Gavin admitted warily. He dared not deny it, since he did not know what the King had been told, or by whom.

'For what purpose?' the King pursued, and then

laughed suddenly: 'Tut, man, you're blushing!' He laid a hand on Gavin's shoulder. 'No need to answer—I can read it in your face clear enough. I should have known: nothing else would have led you to take such a risk for a man of no account. You love the maid. Am I not right?'

'Love is for fools!' retorted Sir Gavin angrily, all his prudent courtesy forgotten in the embarrassment of the moment. The King smiled wryly.

'Would you call your King a fool, my Gavin?'

The quiet voice stirred Gavin to dismay and he sank again to his knees.

'Indeed no, sire,' he protested. 'Forgive me.'

The King laid a hand caressingly on his head.

'I think I know you better than you do yourself,' he said gently. 'Perhaps it's as well, or you'd not leave here today a free man.'

Gavin caught his hand and kissed it, with all the more enthusiasm for the relief he felt.

'You are too good, sire,' he said warmly.

'And a great deal more honest than you, my Gavin,' returned the King. 'Now tell me about this maid—does she look on you with favour?'

Gavin forgot his manners again and frowned.

'She doesn't look on me at all. It was over long ago—though God knows there never was anything to be over,' he added.

'Poor Gavin. She was a bonny wench too—fine eyes—if she'd not been a Papist, and if the circumstances had been different—but there we are.' He dismissed the subject from his mind. 'Come now, we'll take the air in the garden and talk of your marriage. I wonder sometimes if perhaps I was wrong, and it was not after all the match for you—'

Gavin reassured him warmly on that point, and they wandered down to the garden together, the King leaning on his arm. It was clear to everyone who saw them that the rift was healed.

But for all his relief Gavin returned home later that day in a sober mood. If the King had not believed him, if he had not been able to use his charm to good effect, it might have been a serious matter. And someone must have informed on him to the King. He intended to find out who it was.

He remembered the pock-marked man just as Sim asked to see him, his eyes bright with news.

'I followed him, sir—I found where he went.' He paused, then concluded, his eyes on Sir Gavin's face: 'He's my Lady Sidney's man, sir. He went to her house.'

'What do you mean, sir, by bursting in on me in this manner?'

'What do *you* mean, my lady, by setting your spies on me?'

At Gavin's words the anger faded from Lady Philomena's eyes. She turned pale, and then red, and folded her hands firmly in her lap to still their trembling.

'I don't understand you, sir,' she said coldly. 'What do you mean?'

'You understand me very well,' he retorted. 'I was followed this morning all the way home from—a certain house where I had been a guest—'

'From your whore's bed, you mean,' she corrected him, her voice sharp with disgust.

'So that's it!' he exclaimed. 'You want to keep your eye on me when I'm not tied by the heels at your side. You want to make sure that I don't find consolation for a tedious hour or two in any arms but your own. But let me tell you, my lady, that no woman owns me. I am my own man. I go where I choose and I keep the company I choose and I bed where I choose, and no one—not you, nor any other—dictates to me what I do with my time. You had better learn that now, or you'll have cause to rue it.'

Her eyes were hard.

'Oh no, sir. You are mistaken. If you want my money and my name, then I must have you: unconditionally. There are to be no whores in your bed, high-born or otherwise. And no red-haired Papists either to tumble in the grass.'

He stood very still, staring at her, as the words slowly penetrated his brain. It was a moment or two before he realised she was speaking of Honoria. He had a vivid recollection of that sweet and painful scene in the wood at their last meeting. Could Lady Philomena be referring to that? Surely not—it was a coincidence that she had used that expression—

'What do you know of her?' he asked slowly.

'I know you didn't mean a word of all that nonsense you told me of bringing her down, her and her idolatrous kin. That was just a story, to deceive me. It wasn't the priest you were after, or the brother or the aunt, but her. You wanted her white body in your bed so that you could work your foul lusts on her—and she was hot for you, too, don't think I don't know that. Hot and ready—'

He swung his arm down and slapped her, hard, on the cheek, abruptly bringing her words to an end before he had to endure any more of that horrible outpouring of hate and disgust.

'Shut up!' he shouted. 'You foul-mouthed bitch! Mistress Somervell has nothing to do with you—'

'Has she not indeed?' she returned. 'That shows how little you know about it. Proud high-stomached wench that she is, lording it over her betters as if she wasn't as poor as a beggar—and a beggar is what she'll be too when I've finished with her, if she's lucky, that is—'

'What do you mean?' he asked sharply. 'What are you talking about?'

'Do you know how she used me once?' Lady Philomena went on, ignoring his question. 'Her father was dying—another bigoted Papist like herself, he was—and they brought me word of it. As a good neighbour I set out with my chaplain to pay my respects and offer the good man's services at the deathbed. Imagine that, Sir Gavin: even at the eleventh hour I offered the man the chance of salvation—and she spurned me! There in the doorway of the bedroom she stood, and would not let us pass—would not let my chaplain to her father's side, to urge him to repentance, though I pleaded with her most earnestly. Not only that, but when I stood firm she called her servants and—you'll scarcely believe this, Sir Gavin—she ordered her servants to throw us out of the house! As if we were gypsies begging at the door! Can you wonder that I want to see her brought low—lower even than her father, though I don't doubt he's burning in Hell for his sins—'

As she spoke Gavin imagined the scene with appalling clarity: the dying man, surrounded by his loving family, perhaps with a priest in attendance somewhere—and the interfering neighbour disturbing the peace of those final moments, trying to force her way in, to impose her beliefs on a man who had suffered all his life for his faith. He could see Honoria as clearly as if he had been there himself, protective and angry, not caring one jot how much she offended their powerful neighbour, so long as her father might draw his last breath in tranquillity. He almost cried out with admiration for her courage.

Then he remembered something Lady Philomena had said a short while ago: 'a beggar she'll be, too, when I've finished with her—if she's lucky—' His heart stood still, and he looked into those implacable eyes.

'What have you done?' he asked, his voice dangerously quiet. 'What have you done to her?'

'Nothing that she didn't bring on herself,' retorted his betrothed. 'If she has priests in the house what can she expect?'

He felt himself turn cold. Forgetting everything but Honoria's plight he grasped her shoulders and shook her fiercely.

'What have you done? Answer me, woman!'

'Then take your hands off me!'

He did so, and stood back, watching her through narrowed eyes, hard and brilliant as the sapphires she wore at her throat, a present from him. She looked up at him and said coolly:

'She broke the law, Sir Gavin. She invited a priest—a Jesuit, what's more—to conduct her aunt's funeral—'

'Funeral?' he broke in. 'Is her aunt dead?'

'One doesn't generally conduct a funeral for the living,' she retorted. Then she went on: 'As I was saying, she had that same Father Swayne in the house when her aunt died. I thought it was a possibility, so I made it my business to find out when the funeral was to take place, and made sure the pursuivants were ready and waiting. You could have learned a great deal from me that day, sir,' she said with satisfaction. 'We caught him fair and square, and he's now in gaol awaiting trial. And so is little Mistress Somervell—'

'In gaol?' He almost shouted the words.

'No, alas. She's still at home: someone bailed her out. But she'll stand trial, and then there'll be no escape for her. She'll not be so haughty with me again after that. It won't help,' she added maliciously, 'that young Master Blount skipped overseas the moment he was set free. The King won't look on that family with the same favour another time.'

His anger took on a more personal note.

'So it's you I have to thank that news of Master Blount's travels came to the King's ears! And that I nearly found myself on a charge of high treason as a consequence.'

'You?' she demanded, astonished. 'What has it to do with you?'

'Did it not occur to you that I worked to have him released? Of course it has something to do with me. Did you find the thought of being widowed again a diverting one? Or did you decide you'd rather not wed me, and that this was an easy way out?'

She flinched at the ironic tone.

'I had not thought it would affect you,' she admitted.

'Then I'll give you time to think,' he flung at her, moving to the door. 'And if I'm not back in time for our wedding you can take Sir Lionel Talbot instead. I don't imagine you'd care much either way.'

She rose to her feet.

'Where are you going?'

'To Honoria Somervell. To do all in my power to get her out of your clutches.'

'You'll not get the King's help this time.'

He half turned, his lip curling.

'Shan't I? I rather fancy he might not think well of that little scene at her father's deathbed.'

She reddened, and he was thankful she had told him the story: it might prove useful. The King had a kind heart, whatever his views on Catholics, and the in-humanity of Lady Philomena's behaviour would not please him.

'If you go to her,' said his betrothed warningly, 'then I shall not wait for you. I'm not playing second fiddle to a red-haired country wench.'

'Have you not learned by now that you can't hold a candle to her?' he retorted.

He saw her eyes blaze, and her hands move sharply. It was a moment before he realised that she was tugging at the betrothal ring he had placed upon her finger at Christmas time.

She had it off at last, and with all her strength she hurled it at him: it hit the wall behind him and fell tinkling to the floor, where he let it lie.

'Go!' she screamed. 'Go to her and be damned. God alone knows what I ever saw in a selfish whoring hypocrite like you! Get out—get out and never let me see you again!'

He bowed curtly, his mouth set in a hard line.
'With pleasure, my lady,' he said, and left the house.

CHAPTER
SIXTEEN

IT was going to be a beautiful day. When Honoria looked out of her window a milky cushion of mist lay on the meadows beyond the lane, and high over all spread the serene untroubled blue of the summer sky. The air was warm, even at this early hour.

But the beauty of the morning did nothing to ease her aching heart. Her eyes misted with tears as she gazed out on the tranquil scene, and though she swallowed hard and turned to dress herself and make her way downstairs, her mouth was set in the hard line she found necessary to keep it from trembling, and she was weary with sleeplessness. The days were interminably long, but the nights were worse. She rarely slept until the first dawn light crept into her room, and then, very often, she woke late with a crippling headache and crawled miserably through the hours until bed time came round again.

She tried not to think too much of the future. Father Swayne was in prison, and she was charged with harbouring him. That was certain to mean imprisonment for her too. She could see no way of escape, and her courage had never been so low as it was now.

If only she had someone left to turn to: Philip or her aunt, or some other loving friend or relation. But there was no one. Even here at home there was only Tom now for company. Meg and Cook had gone, because she could no longer afford either to pay or to feed them and once she was in prison their plight would be worse. But Tom had refused to go, and there was a little comfort in his steadfast loyalty. If only he were not always as lost in gloom as she.

Sir Gavin was right, she thought, as she slowly descended the stairs. It is foolish to love. If you do not love then no one has power to hurt you. But as soon as you give your heart to another you are within reach of pain. She knew that now: it was all she had left, the tearing anguish inside her that came from loving too much. She missed Philip, and wished for the gentle strength of his friendship, knowing it could never be hers again, and she missed her aunt's loving presence about the house. But the deepest pain of all she dared not think about, for it hurt her too much. It was bound up with an unbearable recollection of strong arms about her, carrying her to safety, of warm lips on hers, of a sunlit glade and a moment close to ecstasy. Though she tried not to remember, these things were part of her still, bound up with the emptiness and despair of the present. What is the point of love, she thought, if it can do all this to you?

As she went into the kitchen she could hear Tom moving about in the stables. He would have breakfasted by now, and was seeing to the needs of their sole remaining horse. There was little enough to keep him busy these days.

She filled a jug with ale and took bread from the crock and carried them through to the parlour, then returned for plates and cups. Even alone as she was she felt she could better face the bleakness of life if she kept up the little surface courtesies, like setting her place at the table, or dressing with care, as she had this morning, in the neat sage-green linen, covered—out of respect for her aunt—by the loose folds of a black taffeta over-gown.

Mechanically, her mind in the dazed sleep-walking state in which she lived for much of the time these days, she placed two wooden trenchers on the table, and the horn beakers beside them, and stood back to see if she had forgotten anything. Another chair, she thought

absently: there is only one, set at my place—why has
Aunt Anne's been moved?

And then the realisation swept her, as never before
until now: Aunt Anne had gone. Never again would she
share the simple meals, sit with her at the fireside, hear
of her joys and sorrows or tell of her own. For ever and
ever now Honoria would be alone, facing the hostility of
neighbours and the inhumanity of the law without
anyone but Tom to stand at her side. She gave one
terrible cry of anguish and sank on to her chair, her head
bent over the table, weeping uncontrollably against her
folded arms. All the misery and grief and bitterness of
the past long weeks, unreleased until now, poured from
her in a flood of despairing tears.

At last, after long desolate minutes, she thought she
heard a sound and slowly raised her head. Wide shafts of
morning sunlight spread from the windows, full of
dancing gold dust, to lie upon the floor in the doorway. Some trick of the light, aided perhaps by the
tear-dimmed mistiness of her eyes, seemed to have
formed a mirage there, as if her grief and loneliness had
conjured up the person she most longed to see. She sat
gazing in blank misery at the shining vision, gold and
blue in the sunlight, strong hands reaching out to her
with a vain promise of comfort.

And then the tears cleared a little from her lashes, and
she saw that the blue silk was stained with dust, the tiny
pearls which patterned it hanging loose in one or two
places, that the blue eyes were deep-set with weariness,
and the corn-gold hair wildly dishevelled. If this was a
vision it was a disconcertingly human one.

Unsteadily, hope and fear conflicting in her, she rose
trembling to her feet and tried to speak, but no words
came. Instead, the apparition moved nearer, out of the
sunlight, and she saw that he was unmistakably real:
alive, breathing, full of concern.

'Honoria,' he said, in that deep resonant voice, 'don't

weep. It's going to be all right.' He faced her across the table and laid his hand, strong and warm, over hers. 'Father Swayne is set free, and they'll drop the charges against you.'

She gave a little inarticulate cry, and then whispered:

'But he can't be . . . How . . . ? Oh, don't play games with me, please, sir . . .'

'I was never more serious in my life,' he said, and she saw that he was frowning a little. Then in the next moment his face cleared and the old lightness returned to his eyes. 'As for your Father Swayne, a little bribery and a word or two in the right place can work wonders.'

In spite of herself she looked a little shocked, and he laughed suddenly. It seemed a long time since she had heard so good a sound.

'Would you rather I left him to his fate? Come now, my dear, you can't have it both ways. Did I not tell you once that I'd cheerfully perjure myself if it suited me?' He moved to perch sideways on the table edge, one leg swinging nonchalantly. 'But I'd not choose to do it too often,' he added. 'You've brought me trouble enough as it is. I can't keep on at this pace: your latest escapade has cost me an exhausting afternoon, a sleepless night and more hours than I care to remember on the road. Still—' He grinned, his eyes merry, 'I think they'll not lightly dare to search my house for Papist priests, or haul my wife to court on a charge of recusancy.'

She felt the colour drain from her face, and then return again, flooding it with crimson.

'What . . . what do you mean . . . ?' she whispered.

He waved a hand with an airy gesture.

'I'm speaking of when we're married,' he said. Honoria stared at him in bewilderment: the world seemed suddenly to have turned topsy turvy. She wondered if she were dreaming all this after all.

'But the Lady Philomena is to be your wife,' she pointed out in a puzzled tone. He shook his head, his smile broadening every moment he sat there.

'Not any longer. She flung her betrothal ring in my face yesterday afternoon. There are still the legal matters to disentangle, but that's a formality. Doubtless she will drag poor Lionel Talbot to the altar in my place. But I am free, and when the dust has settled a little the King will be giving his blessing for a splendid wedding with rather a different bride.' He flicked her cheek lightly with one finger. 'Does that reassure you?'

She wished she did not feel so stupidly dazed, so unable to take in what he was saying. She stood gazing at him, breathing fast, trying to make sense of it all. She supposed this was how those grand court masques ended, when the god descended in his chariot from the clouds to put everything right. But something told her that this was as unreal as the elaborate court entertainments, and as far removed from her life. It was a golden dream of what might be in another more perfect world. She shook her head, the tears starting to her eyes.

'I am a Catholic, Sir Gavin,' she reminded him through a painful obstruction of the throat. She was surprised when he continued to smile as serenely as ever.

'I had noticed,' he said ruefully. 'Is that not why I've spent half my life for the past months extricating you from one desperate situation after another?'

She bent her head and twisted her hands together nervously.

'I am not going to change,' she said.

'I should hope not!' he returned fervently. He slid his hand under her chin and tilted her head so that he could look into her eyes. 'That is exactly why we are to be married, so I can keep you out of harm's way. So no one will ever again vent their hatred on you by persecuting you—as I did once, to my shame. I shall protect you from all that, Honoria.'

'Protect you.' The words, however kindly meant, sent a little chill through her. He held her heart in his hands

and he did not know it: nor, perhaps, would he care if
she were to tell him. Yet she realised how unfair it was of
her to regret that he did not offer her the love she craved.
Once he had wanted only her body, now, at least, some
warmer feeling had woken in him, stirring the pity
natural in a strong and powerful man towards a lonely
and persecuted woman. Perhaps his own sense of guilt at
the harm he had done her once had helped to bring him
here today. I ought to be grateful, she thought, God
knows I need protection. But aloud she said coolly:

'That does not sound like your philosophy, Sir Gavin.
I thought you did not believe in allowing anyone to tie
you down. I cannot think you really want to make
yourself responsible for me. I can give you nothing in
return. 'Except my heart,' said her thoughts, but she
knew that would not interest him.

For a moment he looked faintly surprised, as if he had
not fully realised himself what he was doing.

'No,' he said slowly, 'it doesn't sound like me, does
it?' He smiled, very gently. 'But that is what you have
done to me, Honoria. All my life until now I have shut
out other people and their feelings, unless I could make
use of them in some way. And now all at once I find that
the life I have chosen has no meaning of any kind. It is
empty. Even I, Honoria, need to be tied by something
more than self-interest.'

'So I am to save you from that. I am to let you care for
me so that your life can have some meaning.' Her eyes
were bleak as she spoke, and he looked puzzled.

'Honoria, what's wrong? Do you hate me so much
that you will not even accept my protection? I will
promise to let you alone as far as possible, if that's what
you wish. I shan't force myself on you. But you'll have
my name to protect you, and my wealth and my
influence. It is no small thing.'

'No, I see that,' she said bitterly. 'I'm sure the Fulwells
will rejoice at my good fortune, seeing me as mistress of

Silston at your side. They too know how powerful you are, to their cost.'

He took her hands in his and said with gravity:

'You will not be mistress of Silston, Honoria. Your friends are to come back and live there. I saw them last night and it is all arranged.'

In spite of herself she gave an exclamation of delight.

'Oh, sir, that was generous indeed!' she cried, her face glowing with pleasure. He smiled ruefully.

'I am sorry to disillusion you, but generosity had nothing to do with it. I simply don't relish living cheek by jowl with the Lady Philomena Sidney. Your friends may have that pleasure. No, I fear self-interest still moves me. And I don't lose by it. You've little enough land yourself, but your neighbour to the west is anxious to sell and that is a far better prospect even than Silston. Lower Kilworth will be one of the richest estates in the area—What's wrong?' he asked, as she gave a tremulous laugh.

She shook her head. 'No, you haven't changed,' she said and the amusement faded as quickly as it had come. 'I should have known. I am not even sure about this sudden urge to protect me. Maybe you have other plans—'

'No—' he broke in, 'no, Honoria. Believe me. All I said just now was true. Certainly, I am not a changed man. You will never see me giving everything I have to the poor, or risking my neck as even you have done—except perhaps for you, my dear heart—' She raised her eyes to his face, wondering if she was hearing him correctly. His voice was low and vibrant with emotion as he went on: 'But for you I think I would risk my life and all I have. Call it selfishness if you like, but I need you as I never thought to need anyone. More, even, than I need all the things I have fought for: power and wealth and the King's favour. If I were to lose all those tomorrow I cannot say I would not mind, for I should, very much, but I could face it cheerfully with you at my side. But if I lose you now—if you will not be my wife—then everything I have is as the dust—without meaning or purpose. Perhaps love is only for fools, Honoria, but I think I am glad to be a fool at last—' His face was flushed, his blue eyes deeply serious as they gazed into hers. Her heart leapt, and she bit her lip to keep it from trembling into a smile, because still she did not dare to hope.

'Love—?' she whispered. It was a question, and he answered it.

'Yes, Honoria: I love you as I swore never to love another living soul. More, I think, than I love myself.' He was smiling now, with wry tenderness, and she allowed herself to return the smile, hesitantly, still unsure.

'I . . . I can't believe it . . . why . . . how . . . ?'

'That, my dear heart, I cannot say. It happened, and there we are. I love your courage and your strength and all the good things you are and I am not, but when I've said all that I still have not explained my love for you.' He gazed at her for a moment in silence, and then became all at once severely practical, the emotion almost banished from his voice. 'I cannot force you to marry me, but if you will allow me to take care of you I will try to make sure you have no cause to regret it. I want no other woman, and I want only to do what makes you happy—so you will not have to endure more of my company than you choose. I'll even live apart from you for most of the time if you would prefer it that way. Just so long as you can live peacefully without harrassment.' She read in his eyes what it cost him to make that offer, and tried to speak, but he cleared his throat and went on: 'Perhaps, one day, you might be able to think more kindly of me—even care for me a little . . .' But before he could say any more she had cried out:

'Gavin, don't! I love you—can't you see I love you?'

and she watched the dawning realisation light his face with incredulous joy. He tried to find words, but none came. Then he laughed and sprang from the table and caught her in his arms, and she clung to him, laughing wildly though the tears filled her eyes.

And then his mouth came down on hers, and their bodies melted together in a passionate embrace, as if nothing again would ever come between them.

Much later, when the sun had moved round to lay its warm fingers on the gold and flame of their hair, he drew back a little and raised his head and smiled into her eyes.

'Honoria, my own dear heart, when can you be ready?'

'Ready?' she asked from her resting place against his shoulder.

'We've a dozen miles or so to ride yet,' he explained. 'I told Father Swayne we should be with him today, so that he could marry us.'

She held up her head at that, eyebrows raised, her eyes bright with amusement.

'Did you indeed? That was very presumptuous of you. What if I'd declined to wed you?'

He laughed.

'I suppose I could not imagine you'd refuse so splendid an offer,' he said. 'In any case, I don't think I meant to give you a chance to say no.' He kissed her lightly before she could protest, and added: 'We shall have to endure a fine court wedding, of course, to keep us within the law. But I've no wish to wait till then to make you my wife, not after so long—' He glanced out of the window at the shimmering heat of the garden. 'I hope it stays fine,' he said.

'Why?' she asked. 'I am so happy I don't care what it does.'

'Ah,' he returned in a whisper, 'but it must not rain tonight. There is no shelter in the glade beside the stream, and that is where we shall make our marriage bed—under the stars, together . . .'

She shivered with delight and reached up to kiss him again.

'I am ready, Gavin my love,' she said.

Masquerade
Historical Romances

Intrigue excitement romance

Don't miss
April's
other enthralling Historical Romance title

PIONEER GIRL
by Margaret Pemberton

To the small band of pioneers struggling towards the Rocky
Mountains in the bitter winter of 1846 the chance meeting with
Major Dart Richards is a fateful encounter. And to the
orphaned Polly Kirkham it is especially disturbing. But the
Major has vowed never again to become involved with a
woman, so why does he find himself accompanying them
across the icy wastes in pursuit of an ideal?

Masquerade
Historical Romances

Intrigue
excitement
romance

THE DANGEROUS GODDESS
by Rose Hughes

'*You're not like other women, my dangerous goddess. You're much too beautiful. Men will rob for you, kill for you . . .*'
On arrival in India Miranda Coulson is forced to recall these fatal words of a fellow passenger as she is met, not by her fiancé, but by the sardonic Captain Adam Redmond, who brusquely tells her to take the next ship home . . .

MASTER OF HERRINGHAM
by Julia Murray

Alicia and Kit Kenyon are stunned to discover that their recently deceased brother has gambled away their family home. They find themselves the tenants of Major Andrew Harbury, a man who both puzzles and provokes Alicia . . .

Look out for these titles in your local paperback shop from
14th May 1982